MONSTER AND THE JEWEL THIEF

CYNDI FARIA

Author's Note the Reader

When I first learned of the amazing author Eve Langlais and her FUC world, I fell hard for her quirky community and zany characters. I may have even shouted FUCN'A a few times reading. Never did I imagine my story idea would be accepted and I'd get to write alongside some of my favorite authors! Dreams do come true, and I'm so happy they did. <3

Thank you so much for spending time with Monster and Pandora on their quest to a HEA...as well as kicking some donkey hee-haw! I can't wait to bring you more Mutant and Mayhem stories, which will only be available in Eve Langlais' FUCN'A world.

Love, hugs, and happy reading, Cyndi.

Acknowledgments

Beta Read by Rachel Rawlings

Copy Edits by Brandi Salazar, Editing Done Write

Proofread by Devin Govaere

Cover by Rebecca Poole with Dreams2Media

To the reader who sings praises about her newest book boyfriend like they're soulmates, I pledge to make all my beasty heroes swoon-worthy just for you. ~ Cyndi Faria 😌

Monster Johnson stomped a path toward his new assignment, irritation from cutting short his international mission barely concealed. The special ops agent for the Furry United Coalition didn't take kindly to the higher-ups ordering him to return to FUC. Not when he'd been hot on the heels of the mad scientist, mastermind Dr. Ichabod Crick, aka DIC, the man who'd kidnapped, experimented on, and ruined Monster's life. He could no more hide the anger blazing hot in his cheeks than he could his desire for revenge.

But what were his choices? Orders were orders. Whether he liked them or not.

At least he'd been assigned to work with Director Alyce Cooper of the Furry United Coalition Newbie Academy, FUCN'A. They'd once teamed up on a secret mission deep in the Amazon rainforest, and Monster considered the woman a top-notch mentor and director. Monster's instructions had been to meet up with the llama shifter, who'd direct him to a newly created Coping class for wayward and exper-imented-upon, hard-to-handle newbies.

The key factor he focused on wasn't the class, however. There was an experimental survivor like himself, and Monster took it as his chance to return–with a secret agenda he'd keep to himself for the time being.

Knowing firsthand what the evil DIC did to his victims gave Monster the upper hand. He was confident enough to believe he could connect with the Experimental Juvenile Active Cadet (EJAC). Confident enough to squeeze every last ounce of information from this shifter if given the chance.

Monster pressed his shoulders back, catching his full reflection in one of the hallway's seven-foot-tall glass display cases. His dark hair was as unruly as he suspected his new students would be. But he'd handled worse. Even though nerves threatened, his imposing stature kept most from challenging him, a trait he counted on to keep the students from challenging him. Still, he gave his neck a pop, working out the built-up tension.

Yes, Monster believed he would prove to the students that, with hard work and determination, they could turn their nightmarish idea of a future into something that could benefit society, like he had, hunting for DIC and taking out his accomplices along the way. Which was a good reason to take a hiatus from his outstanding mission. He needed a break in his case, and his intuition told him something was amiss within the walls of the FUCN'A.

His first task at hand was to meet his students and settle into the Academy atmosphere—one he was familiar with. Nothing he couldn't handle. Six weeks tops. Then, if his leads dried up, he'd return to his mission in South America.

Though his outer wounds had healed, Monster's right hand was left disfigured. When he shifted, his monstrous shape was no more definable as a gorilla shifter than animal parts sticking out of a human-sized ball of putty. He was colloquially called a Lump.

Still, he was a kickass ball of goo who would destroy the man who did this to him. Even Monster's life expectancy had been reduced. But he was alive and still kicking four years later. Most Lumps—those shifters who didn't have a full animal form—didn't survive beyond one year.

Maybe his anger fueled him. He counted on it. The sooner he located DIC, the sooner he'd settle up. Force the man to reverse the experiment. Find the cure to the chimera DNA he carried. Continue his mission of protecting the innocent from men like DIC.

"Are you ready to meet your students?" Alyce wore a lavender power suit, which made her dark skin glow and showcased her straight, black hair.

But he wasn't fooled by her feminine exterior. Alyce was tall—a foot shorter than him—and she wasn't a woman to be messed with. Monster shook her hand, giving it a squeeze to let her know he was glad to be working with her again after nearly four years.

"After you." She motioned to the closed door, the windowpane giving a glimpse of the ten FUCN'A students, including the one rescued experiment—a Lump like Monster. She lifted a thin carrot to her lips, took a bite, and chewed around the carrot bits she was working between her teeth. "We believe this case is tied to yours... I did obtain personal school records from Principal Epona, who's returned from overseeing the primary grades to elementary school levels, so she can have more time to run her equine rescue. There might be information I'm not seeing via one-page transcripts. Let's hope this new survivor lives longer than a year."

Monster's chest tightened while Alyce blinked her

emotions. The young man was about the same age Monster had been when he'd been kidnapped. A normal lifetime ahead of him, ripped away by a madman. Alyce and Monster's mother had been close friends. After his mother's death right after Monster had been experimented on, Alyce looked in on him, and they'd formed a tight relationship, fused enough that she was aware of his vendetta against DIC. "I'll teach the new shifter about revenge. That ought to give him a reason to live."

Alyce touched Monster's arm with her free hand and added a discerning glare. "Miranda contacted me. If she wants you here, she has a good reason. Teach Willy Tagger, the new Lump, to trade revenge for justice and help him grow a negative into a positive."

Positive, smoshitive. Monster knew damn well why he'd been summoned. FUC Agent Miranda Brownsmith knew something she wasn't willing to share via Alyce, but if Alyce's cadets were in trouble, she'd be invested. It didn't matter where his orders came from. Monster needed to gain this kid's trust. The mission overseas had put him no closer to DIC than the day Monster had escaped the crude laboratory, and all involved were growing impatient.

Willy, who'd be attending cadet training, held possible answers. He'd had an eerily similar experience to Monsters. The young man was kidnapped off the street within the town of Willow Wisp. From looking at Willy's file, he'd miraculously escaped and was picked up by FUCN'A. Willy was lucky to be alive. Monster was lucky he had a potential first-hand lead.

A grin spread on Monster's face, and hope stirred in the pits of his belly. One solid clue would help him match the name he recalled when he'd been kidnapped to a face, so he could formally identify the bastard and take down DIC for good.

That was if he could stay focused knowing his ex-lover—that sweet little crow shifter Pandora Raven—lived a short mile from the Academy.

"You see what I'm seeing?" Alyce peered closer through the rectangular window in the door and popped the remaining end of the carrot into her mouth.

Monster joined Alyce at the window, feeling as if he'd been cloned and gut-punched looking at Willy, a kiss of kinsmanship kicking up inside him. The twenty-something-year-old male had been a gorilla shifter, like Monster was, before he was kidnapped and experimented on.

The young male wore a ball cap and glasses, and his shoulders were slumped, making his bulked-up stature appear smaller.

Monster knew the guarded pose intimately. Make yourself insignificant. Avoid eye contact. Trust no one. "I agree with you. DIC's work. But why target gorilla shifters?"

It was a new similarity, the first in nearly half a decade he tried to wrap his mind around.

"You'll figure it out. But like I warned earlier, Willy needs time to heal and someone to teach him that his life as an experimental survivor isn't over yet." Alyce cracked the door.

If it was the same scientist, he could be local, which was why Monster's leads led to dead ends. "If this is DIC's work, the kid could have longer to live than a few more months."

"I'm aware of a special task force trying to figure out if targeting gorilla shifters is the missing lead, but until I learn more, get to know the kid. He's not talking. He needs someone to trust to help him remember key details. Give him a reason to thrive instead of shutting down and waiting to die."

Monster cleared his throat, craving to be on that investigative side. There, rather than teaching behind a desk. But orders were orders. Even if the flashback of being inside walls like these hit him hard and nostalgia stirred in his heart. He'd met Pandora at the Willow Wisp Elementary School when his future was wide open and everything about the two of them had been viewed from behind rose-colored glasses. Then later, they'd paired up briefly as new cadets at the Academy.

He entered the room, his boots landing heavily on the tiled floor, but the shock of seeing the whiteboard or the desk facing the rows of students wasn't what shook him.

He could still picture Pandora, her feathered, black hair tied up in pigtails, blinking lashes his way, shooting him a perky pout, that naughty little crow shifter who stole his heart. Hell, who still owned his heart, even if she'd forgotten all about him.

Like he'd told her to do. It was the right choice. Why fall in love when his days were numbered? He'd become the one holding her back from finding a worthy mate, one whose DNA hadn't been corrupted. He stood by his resolve to hunt DIC for as long as he had on this earth.

Monster had been a jerk back then. He'd gone and broken Pandora's heart when he'd decided to hunt the lunatic who'd tortured him instead of settling down with Pandora. For a damn good reason.

A special agent with a loved one or family had a weak spot some DIC-wannabe could use as leverage to lure Monster into being recaptured. So, he'd cut ties with Pandora to keep her safe. Another reason he stood by.

Which was why he'd asked his superiors for a mission

that would take him far from FUCN'A and the nearby town of Willow Wisp. He had lacked the strength to face the disappointment behind Pandora's loving brown eyes every time she caught him obsessing over clues that could lead to his revenge. So he laid out his reasoning, both their hearts breaking in the process, and her telling him she loved him enough to let him go.

His throat constricted from the emotions and regret he still carried. He'd never stopped loving her, but for Pandora, to keep her safe, he'd made the choice for both of them, telling her she should forget him and move on. Now that he'd returned, he only needed to get through these next six weeks behind the secure walls of the Academy so his and Pandora's paths wouldn't cross. He'd done four years. He could do the time, even if, inside, regret soured his stomach and he felt like he was dying.

Alyce cupped her hand over Monster's shoulder. "You got this. I have faith in you."

Alyce had taken Monster under her wing when he'd been found and brought to FUCN'A. Now it was Monster's turn to give back. If he got lucky and uncovered information from Willy, Monster just might cash in on his revenge.

A chair smashed into the door with a deafening *whack*.

Monster jumped, taking only a moment to rush to the back of the room. He grabbed the mongoose shifter by the nape, her eyes bulging, and the coiled cobra shifter by the throat, holding the two midair. "This isn't *National Geographic*. I have no patience for this shit."

The mongoose *bark-squeaked* before transforming back into her human form. "Hey. Let me go. Slimy Slithering has it out for me."

Hisss. The snake's tongue darted out between fangs, and

he coiled his tail around Monster's feet, attempting to trip the instructor.

"Return to your human form, snake, or I'll lock you in an aquarium and feed you crickets for the rest of your life. Do it now," Monster ordered.

As if a deflating balloon, the cobra quivered, and his wide neck shrunk. Two hands wrapped around Monster's forearm. "You're choking me."

Monster shoved the nude male forward, tempering a smirk. If he was honest, he enjoyed youth and the fire that brewed within them. An innocence that had been stolen from him. "Not in my class. You've been warned. Both of you get dressed and retake your seats."

"That was quite a welcome. But let's not destroy the instructor on day one." Alyce patted Monster on the back and took a seat at the rear of the class, eager to introduce him. "This is Special Ops Agent Monster Johnson. His background is not unlike your own. He'll be your instructor for the next month and a half. Pay attention. Some of you might even become future agents if you don't kill each other first."

Monster huffed as he measured each individual, identifying with their wide-eyed and glossy gazes. The class was composed of five females, five males. All in their early twenties. Still moldable. He hoped.

Monster took his place at the front of the class, hitching his leg on the corner of the desk, praying he wouldn't come off as some know-it-all asshole instructor, the kind he'd hated as a newbie. What he wanted to say and what perched on his lips warred. But Alyce's pep-talk won in the end. "Some of you are feeling out of control. Scared. You may be a little fragile. But less like the petals of a dahlia. More like a stick of dynamite. But there's a place for you here and abroad. If you can learn to control that rage, that power, and your newfound abilities, and stop blaming others for your difficulties in life, you, too, can find self-acceptance and purpose again, gaining a life of happiness."

A hand shot up in the back. "Hi, I am Daisy. That's easier said than done. Just look at Mary Mongooski and Lawerance Kai. Those two are natural enemies. We're all hopeless. There's no changing that. Every time I sneeze, I shift into an ass with an attitude. My donkey shifter form is ready to buck and bite at first glance. To top it off, I'm allergic to grass."

What had Alyce signed him up for? The Detention Club? Monster glanced out the line of windows, noting the meadow and bits of cottonwood pollen floating in the air and filtering through the window screen.

Coping with new abilities was all about making modifications. He withdrew his handkerchief from his pocket and handed it to the allergy-cursed donkey shifter, motioning to the newbie to put it over her mouth and nose, like a makeshift mask. "Thanks for the warning. I'll help you with controlling your transitions. Trust me."

"This cloth isn't going to stop me from..." Her head fell forward, and she started to whuffle, sleep finding her quickly.

The director stayed planted in her seat.

Monster noted Alyce lifted a brow, as if she were impressed with the chloroform trick she'd taught Monster to use during his Threat in Training (TiT) course. "Anyone else a threat to their classmates that I need to know about? I won't take chances with anyone's safety."

Snorts, grunts, and hisses echoed. Willy slumped in his seat, resting his chin on his knees.

Monster waited patiently. He was a patient man, after all, and that could be said about waiting for the right lead and capturing DIC. But first, he wanted to speak with the EJAC to learn if Willy might remember any hint of information about his captor.

Willy didn't divulge even a sigh. Just sat in his seat, leg jiggling, head down, hands folded.

He feared these walls just like Monster had after he'd been kidnapped and had returned to live among the other shifters. Willy's PTSD was palpable within the confines of the room, his respiration picking up and fogging his green-lensed glasses. Monster didn't know the cadet from Adam. He didn't trust him at this point. For all Monster knew, he could have been planted by the evil DIC.

Sadly, Monster realized he didn't have enough to go on. Not yet. But in time… Monster checked his wristwatch. Ten minutes down. Already one lesson under their belts. "Ready for your first assignment?"

The EJAC's head popped up, and he held Monster's gaze briefly with those dark brown eyes. "I don't know anything. Someone was tailing me in Willow Wisp before I was kidnapped. I called Bonafide Security (BS) when I suspected I was being followed to the Academy and got FUC'd, for all the good it did. I was kidnapped in town in broad daylight—after that, I don't remember much of my escape except running. I still don't know where I escaped from because my mind is cloudy. But FUCN'A found me, luckily, before the human police. I'm still healing after being stitched up. I haven't shifted to my Lump form or my gorilla form since before I woke up here. All I need is to learn control so I can go after the person who did this to me. The sooner, the better. What's with the assignment already?"

At least the student was talking, his rage slipping past his control. Especially after he'd contacted BS and had gotten the runaround. Another similarity between them—both craving validation and vindication.

On a physical level, Monster wanted to see if the EJAC was like himself, but not in class. Not with innocents around him. One wrong shift could be deadly.

If anything, Monster was ultra-protective of innocent people. He darted his gaze to Daisy, still lost in slumber. "Lesson One: Honesty will cost you."

The entire class twisted in their seats and stared at the donkey shifter, still puffing breaths and carried off to la-la land by the drug-laced hanky.

The EJAC slumped, recapturing his timid pose.

Maybe how Monster had tricked Daisy wasn't the right first lesson. Or maybe it was. But facts were facts: sharing vulnerabilities with a stranger could get you killed. And the last thing Monster wanted filed against him was a stack of Complaints on Campus (COC) forms. "I'm here to help you through these next six weeks. Tomorrow's class will be held outside in the quad. I want to see what I'm dealing with, shift-wise. I need each of you to witness Lesson Two."

Another hand rose, halfway, elbow bent. Shaky and cautious. "When is the test starting?"

They were learning already not to trust the person they thought they could. That was exactly how the one who'd trapped Monster had led him to his doom. These students were shifters by nature. But the EJAC had his nature twisted in the worst way. Monster needed to prove to Willy that he could and would survive this transition. And better to do so with someone who he could relate to, and Monster certainly did. "Now."

The girl in the red sweater chirped a high-pitched sound.

Monster twitched while identifying the pitch—a cheetah

or some kind of fowl. At least in the Amazon, he knew the apex predators. Good thing he was one.

He picked up the dry-erase pen and wrote on the board, his mangled hand managing the pen, modifying the way he held the tool. "Question number one: Tell me what you want to get out of this class and what you want from me, personally."

The EJAC met Monster's gaze, staring down at his own twisted right hand, his mind clicking the pieces together. They were alike. Maybe even linked by their natural and mutually manufactured DNA. Monster had lived longer than the suspected year that non-full-animal EJACs were cursed with.

After twenty minutes, Monster collected papers, but when he approached the Lump's chair, within the time Monster had turned his back, the EJAC had disappeared right from under his nose. Same as Monster had done that first day with Alyce.

When Monster strolled to Daisy's desk, he cut the donkey shifter some slack, letting her wake on her own time.

Alyce met Monster at the door, blocking it, noticing his rush to find Willy. "Let the kid go. Willy is trying to forget his attacker. Trying to cope like you had to do. You know it's as rough for him as it was for you. But in time, if he lets you in, he may recall and share the details needed to solve his case."

And Monster's case. "Cope. The kid's done with the bullshit. Fights breaking out in his own classroom surely ignited his PTSD. To cure that he's going to have to face his fears. He wants revenge. I'm going to help him find it."

Alyce imposed her stature, crowding him. "Willy needs justice."

"Justice my ass." Monster clutched his middle finger from escaping. He knew better than to blame Alyce for his anger when he was pissed at himself. Still… "His life's been cut short. He's an unnatural being. Angry."

"Teach him patience," the llama shifter hummed.

Monster blew a tired breath. He was dragging tail after his return trip from South America, hips aching from the minuscule plane seats that failed to accommodate his girth, even sitting in first class. Eyes starting to burn and vision blurring from pushing himself, he didn't argue. He shelved Alyce's request for the time being.

"That wasn't so hard."

Alyce *was* right. He needed to give the kid time to adjust to his new reality just as Alyce had done for him. Then he'd pounce. He had hurt people he cared about, and Alyce could read Monster like the back of her manicured hand. "Fine. But if I've learned anything in the field, it's that I can't just let the kid hide. He'll never become a contributing member of society that way."

"I understand." Alyce took the lead, the two eventually walking side by side down the empty corridor of the Academy. "But powers above have a task force on the EJAC's case. I don't want you taking on a case that's too personal just yet. Focus on teaching coping skills, self-acceptance, and a fulfilling future, not how you got the way you are or the negative aspects. I can't have you slipping up."

Alyce meant not again. She couldn't risk Monster screwing up a mission like he had the first and last time he caught wind of DIC. A specific mission he'd failed at identifying a previous case and an escapee from one of Mastermind's labs. Monster believed but couldn't prove he and DIC had certainly interacted and crisscrossed paths on multiple occasions.

Monster rubbed his tired eyes.

"I want to talk to you about accommodations while you're here." Alyce motioned up ahead.

Still locked on his past cat-and-mouse with DIC, Monster was just as irritated that DIC had slipped through his hands, as were the nutcase's victims. A regret he wouldn't allow to happen again. That was a promise Monster made to himself. He'd learned to remain focused during his overseas missions. No matter what the task, he'd always hit his mark. In fact, he'd exceeded his supervisor's expectations.

Which gave Monster an idea. On-site at the Academy, he was closer to the task force working the new case. All he needed was to get into their files, re-examine the information. New information they'd obtained in Willy Tagger's case. Because he'd been brought in to teach a class per Alyce's instructions and not to investigate Willy's case.

He schooled the grin attempting to expose his plan. With his new access credentials as a teacher *and* agent on campus, he possessed the means he needed.

Alyce wouldn't buy any games though, no matter his relationship with his mentor. Monster had to appease the director to satisfy Miranda and the higher-ups. If he allowed the director to toss him leads, however, Monster had the potential to capture DIC, who clearly was still or back in the area. "I haven't slept in twenty-four hours. Point me in the direction of Academy housing and a meal. I have a class to teach tomorrow and need to prepare."

"Academy housing is full." Alyce drew a card from her pocket and set it into Monster's hand. "There's only one room available. The B&B isn't far from the Academy, just a modest commute to the town of Willow Wisp. Please, don't let your emotions get in the way of this working out, or you'll be sleeping in your truck."

Alyce was full of warnings tonight, which Monster would have argued if he had energy to protest. He glanced at the business card. A bouquet of flowers sat on a bedside table, and the tagline of the bed and breakfast emblazoned on the card read: *Pandora's Box is waiting to make all your dreams come true.*

A shudder ran through Monster, nearly knocking him back a full foot. Although he couldn't tell if it was due to fear or desire. Fear of facing the one person he'd caused immeasurable pain when he left and the possibility of doing it all over again by coming home. Pandora ran a B&B, apparently. Desire stirred and would quickly destroy him once he spotted her.

She was his kryptonite. She'd be the distraction he couldn't afford. Not with the new EJAC needing his attention, teaching a class, and infiltrating Academy files. "There must be room on campus. In the gym? One of the newbie bunks."

Alyce pinned Monster with a look that threatened him not to challenge the sleeping arrangements–or any order that Alyce handed him, since she was backed by Miranda. "I get a whiff of a COC form en route to my desk, and I'll ask Miranda to put you on a mission hunting snipes."

Fucking perfect. Alyce was pulling the tough-love card. But Alyce had sentenced Monster to six weeks of living hell. Pandora was beautiful with her seductive, dark eyes, that long, black hair that cascaded down her back, those heavenly curves gripping him in all the wrong places.

Or the right places. But his desire for her would put her in danger if they were to rekindle what they'd once had. Not to mention, it would put both of them in harm's way with him thinking about her twenty-four-seven.

She was the one woman Monster hated because she served as puppet-master to his thoughts, the one person he couldn't get out of his mind, no matter how hard he tried. She reminded him that love and revenge would never mix.

She was also the one person he'd learned lesson number one from. His honesty had cost him Pandora. Her love. Her heart. Every single part of their relationship he'd loved.

But now it was time to pay the piper. Face her and all the baggage that came with it. Monster only hoped she didn't take one look at him and kick him to the curb. With his luck, those outside the *supposed* Animal Rescue Special House of Learning—ARSHOL—community would find out they *had* a monster in their town and gun him down or hire the mad DIC to recapture and torture him all over again.

TWO

"Pandora, Monster is headed your way, and he's not happy about it," Alyce's singsong voice burst from the receiver.

Pandora's heart fell a few inches in her chest. But the arrangement she'd made with the FUCN'A director was twofold. "Well, I'm not happy about it either, but a deal is a deal. I'll do this for you, and when the time comes, you'll play your part in what we discussed."

"I won't break my promise unless you break yours," Alyce grumbled under her breath, and then the call went dead.

Which was just fine with Pandora Raven. There was a monster headed to her house, and he happened to be her ex. Or rather Monster Johnson, special ops agent, would arrive in the next few minutes. Alyce was doing her best to protect the man she treated like a son. And if Pandora knew anything, it was the passion behind being a parent.

Her heart leaped into her throat as she realized it was up to her to provide a place for Monster to rest his tired mind, food to nourish his hulky body, and homestyle comforts for the next six weeks. Fuckin' A, she was doomed to fail.

Six weeks. She had a problem, a secret, and no idea how she would keep it buckled inside her. A secret and anger that still felt as fresh as the day Monster had left town. But she was a strong, independent woman. She would have become an agent if…

She blotted her stinging eyes and shoved her emotions down deep where they belonged. She and Monster were over, and she had no business involving herself with him on anything more than a professional level. She could keep her mind and hands to herself, even if her dreams still included snippets of their past romance. She and Alyce had even shaken hands on their agreement.

Tires on the gravel upped her angst.

Both she and Monster had set out to graduate from FUCN'A. She had plans to become a FUC agent in lieu of working as a crow shifter for the Avian Soaring Society (ASS) since she admired Jessie—an ASS member turned FUC agent. She thought she and Monster would get married and live outside the Academy to help the local furries when they weren't on assignment as FUC agents or otherwise involved within the disguised ARSHOL.

She'd even imagined they'd unite as husband and wife, team up for international adventures. Missions abroad and solving cases that involved the furry kind had been her number-one bucket list item.

Until everything changed when Monster had been kidnapped and experimented on. His focus had twisted in on both of them, and he was never the same. Especially after his mother passed. Her heart was destroyed because she'd lost her son.

Pandora had gone through changes of her own, though. Alone. She would never speak ill of a special ops agent. They were acutely impressive and invariably skilled, both physically and mentally. But when she was all alone in the quiet evenings or a lull in the morning, she resented Monster. Yes, more than she cared to admit.

Initially, no matter her determination to show him how much she had loved him, their relationship suffered. Then he found a lead that triggered a memory of the man who'd turned him into a Lump. Monster broke off their relationship in exchange for a secret mission. No explanation other than he'd made the decision to leave for the both of them. And now he was back, his apparent freedom to enter her world without so much as a heads-up seemed as commonplace as breathing for him, but not for her.

Pandora made fists at her side, angry that the memory could still ruffle her feathers. But she resolved in the silence of her suffering. There was a bigger picture now, one Monster was unaware of, and another she would never let down.

She set to work on getting Monster's bed made up, folding the sheets in military corners, and mumbled under her breath, "Squawkin' A."

She fluffed the downy pillow one last time, her feet weighted to the area rug as if she'd been handcuffed to the headboard. "You're okay, Pandora. Six weeks…"

A jeweled pendant necklace lay under the nightstand.

The woman who'd left the B&B the day before held a strong community position and needed a one-night stay while her home was under construction. Pandora knew far too well what it was like wrestling contractors while juggling a full-time job working in a construction zone. It was the least Pandora could do—providing the woman with a night of respite.

Pandora—Dora as she was called by her friends—hadn't prodded on whether the woman would return. It was none of her business that the woman had scampered off as soon as Alyce Cooper entered. She was an imposing woman, usually social and friendly, but that day she'd radiated serious llama vibes.

Pandora had almost expected Alyce to break out with kicks and spits. Without questioning her guest, Pandora turned her attention toward helping Alyce.

She shivered and rubbed a thumb over the shiny ruby, the smooth surface sparkling under the overhead light but failing to provide Pandora with a sense of calm. She could have spent a minute examining the fine stone encased in the pendant if she had time. Instead, she pocketed the stone in her jeans, promising to call the guest in the morning.

On the nightstand sat an empty wine glass that she tucked into her apron pocket and elbow polished the dried condensation until the bureau shined. If anything, she was known for an impeccable house. The saltbox-style exterior with dormer windows, which she'd renamed Pandora's Box and Breakfast after the previous owner sold her the home, was one of her pride and joys.

She couldn't say that her heart was in as good standing.

Monster had left on a mission after he'd broken up with her. His excuse, in her opinion, had been a copout to progressing their relationship. Instead of growing from his situation and turning it into a positive, he'd done the opposite and held on to his anger.

She spread the blinds, peering out at Monster, who roughly tossed his backpack over his shoulder.

Anger and revenge didn't belong in her world.

She told herself she wasn't interested in rushing back into his arms or his bed. Even if Alyce had talked her into providing Monster with a place to lay his thick head. Alyce had her own reasons for wanting Monster to return to the

FUCN'A, she suspected. Reasons the director didn't explain to her. But then Alyce wasn't obligated to explain anything about Pandora's old world and Monster's current assignment.

As soon as these next weeks were over, Monster would disappear behind the gates of the Academy or be sent off on another mission. If she was lucky, he'd never return. She hadn't been ready for his return nor how it twisted her up inside.

She punched the pillow, barely releasing the anger of his betrayal, then strolled out into the foyer, spotting the blue-eyed hunk of nature looming on the threshold.

She thought her heart couldn't plummet any lower, but it plunged to her feet, making her head swim with nostalgia and yearning for their unattainable past.

Monster's skin radiated a slight green hue, and his biceps reminded her of the Swiss Alps she'd read about in the *AAA* magazine. The peaks and valleys that landscaped his form were ordered in a way human muscles didn't grow. But his mountainous shape spoke of his agility and strength, his fitness. Jeans hugged the swell of his thick thighs and brutish form. A simple tee gloved his upper body.

But the set of his jaw revealed little about his heart.

"I brought you flowers. Your favorite kind, tulips."

The tremble and emotion laced through his voice touched her soul, and her traitorous core clenched from his patchouli scent. She shifted as discreetly as she could, scissoring her ankles and hating how his mere presence affected her.

A tiny twitch of pleasure tipped the corner of his mouth.

Yes, Monster was an observant man, down to the fine details. He obviously picked up on the butterflies flitting inside her belly, her racing pulse, and quickening breath stirring up memories. But he'd left her so easily, trading her for his obsession with revenge and destroying any future they could have had.

With Monster standing before her, she felt as if a hornets' nest had exploded in the foyer.

She faked a smile, giving herself credit for effort. "Monster, welcome to Pandora's B&B."

His gaze fell to her sandaled feet, roamed over her denim-covered legs, trailed to where her apron gathered at her waist, and hung momentarily at the spill of flesh that protruded from her corseted bodice before meeting her stare.

It was a predatory gaze, something he'd gained from DIC, who'd changed him.

And it lit her soul on fire.

Damn him. Damn him and DIC, who'd ruined him, them, and a future she still secretly held on to.

"You haven't changed a bit." He entered her space and darted his tongue between his lips, wetting them slightly. He lifted his empty hand, his fingers lingering near her cheek, a hairsbreadth away from her skin.

She ignored the pulse of desire his hot breath against her face caused. The hint of the man who once would have done anything to kiss her was gone. But their attraction was as intoxicating and undeniable as it had ever been.

When he widened his smile, perhaps noticing the flush of cheeks, he wasn't wrong in reading her. She still carried a place in her heart for Monster. Not that she planned to act on it.

She was as strong as she'd ever been. Both in her resolve to survive the next few weeks and to get over him quicker than she had the first time.

She was a crow shifter, after all, with talents of her own. But she *had* changed in ways he couldn't know or measure with his acute sensory abilities. She was wiser. More guarded. She'd dated occasionally, but she'd never let another man get as close as Monster had. She wouldn't survive that pain of losing someone she had loved and lost to madness again. And losing herself wasn't an option... "Let me show you to your room."

"Not even a nice to see you or a thank you for the flowers?" Monster spoke as he followed Pandora.

Was he joking? Four years without so much as a *how are you?* and he thought tulips would patch Pandora's wounds? She whirled, facing him and taking the bait he wiggled at her. She gripped the bouquet, expecting a prick of a thorn that didn't come. "I didn't ask for flowers. I'm doing this as a...favor to Alyce. Not for you. You made the decision for both of us that it was over, so there's no need for chitchat. Room and board are all I'm providing while you're here in town. I have my own life now."

His face hardened, and he set his chiseled jaw. "If that's how you feel, I'll stay out of your way. You don't owe me anything."

It hurt her to be so honest, the pain growing inside her chest as if her heart had exploded and lava burst forth. As her go-to, she kept her hands busy, worrying her fingers over the pendant she'd tucked into her pocket so her mind wouldn't draw her down into a spiral of sorrow. "I'll show you to your room. Then I must return to my duties."

She hustled to where she kept the vases, drew one from the curio, filled it with tepid water, and added a teaspoon of sugar. The honey-fragrant flowers looked nice on the dining room table. But it was the heat welling in Monster's gaze that singed her cheeks and her backside as she ignored the unease of his scrutiny. She no longer had time or patience for courtship games and flirtations or pleasantries. Not with running a business. Not with her full-time responsibilities. "This way…"

He trudged after her, holding back a few paces.

The room was the only one with a king-sized bed. The only room in the house that wasn't currently occupied for the night. And, unfortunately, directly adjacent to her private boudoir.

Tentatively, she entered, finding a loose penny that nearly matched the carpet and stuffing it into her pocket. With a day like today, she needed all the luck she could find before she let loose her true feelings and began to *squawk* the discomfort that Alyce had put both of them in.

The *tick-tick-tick* of a school bus engine and the *hisssss* of the brakes briefly captured Pandora's attention.

"We need to talk, Pandora. A lot has happened since I left."

He didn't even know half of it. The bus driver of the upper elementary students, Mr. Duke, exited the bus and then guided the students down the steps as they dispersed into the neighborhood, while Pandora prayed her little surprise remembered he was riding the Just B4 pre-kinder-garten bus headed to Grandma's after school.

She certainly wasn't going to blurt out that she and Monster shared a son in the first few minutes since Monster's return. If he wanted anything more, including knowledge of Parker, he'd have to earn it tenfold. "You'll sleep here."

A bed with an ornate headboard sat against the far wall. The bathroom was to the right. A sofa faced a fireplace that flickered flames of gold and orange. A woven rug separated the sofa from the hearth. Wood poked from a metal bucket. It was a nice room. The nicest in the B&B.

But where Pandora had considered the house a home, she realized that it was missing something: her other half. Her stronger and more driven half—the only man she'd ever loved. "This room shares a bathroom with the one next door. Remember to lock both doors before you shower. You don't want to flash the human residents and have to get COOCHI involved."

"So that's it. You're worried about Corrective Outdoors Shift or Calming of Humans Incidents. Hence, lock the doors." Monster scouted the space and then jammed his knuckles into his hips. "Believe me, the last thing I want is to reconnect. I won't be here long. I'm so close to finding out who's behind the experiments, I can almost taste it. A new EJAC spouted up. Higher-ups and Alyce want me to work with the newbie. I just need a little more time."

"Time," she shrieked, and her quills bristled her skin, appearing like she had an instant case of pocks. He was as cold as she'd ever seen him. Perfect. But that didn't stop her from feeling something for him. "It's been four years. Four long years since you walked out on me." *On us...*

There it was. The truth behind her blistering anger. Monster had been so wrapped up in his own pain, he'd failed to see that she was vulnerable, pregnancy hormones racing through her veins, her belly growing, and him leaving the taste of his manufactured mission to fall sour in her mouth.

He'd put his revenge before his love for her and, by that choice, his potential love for their child.

Monster dropped his arms, his confliction prominent in his blue-eyed gaze.

At least his eyes hadn't changed. No matter what he

said, she was certain he kept her at a distance for other reasons—like keeping her safe from the monster he saw himself as.

She couldn't know if his mind had stabilized or reversed course. She hadn't learned from anyone at FUC, including Alyce, why Monster had been pulled back to the Academy, although this new EJAC must be the reason.

"I know what I did to you, Dora. You don't know how sorry I am. I don't know if I'll ever get the chance to make it up to you 'cause I'm certain DIC is here. I'm convinced, maybe even someone from Willow Wisp. I feel something in my gut telling me that DIC is going to strike again, close to home—and he appears to be targeting gorilla shifters."

Targeting gorilla shifters? The blood from Pandora's face drained, and her belly twisted into knots of apprehension. The thought of Parker being in danger caused her belly to roil as their baby had inside her. But Monster would never understand her protectiveness over Parker. Nor the way she cared for him even before he was born.

Monster hadn't witnessed her joy in noticing the first flutters of little kicks? He hadn't observed the pain of birthing their son. He hadn't watched the flicker of disappointment in Parker's expression when other dads showed up at school to pick up their child.

No. Pandora was Parker's protector, and he was her world. The last thing she wanted was to jump into a co-parenting relationship with Monster. But if their child's safety was at stake, she'd certainly reach out to Alyce to confirm what she'd heard. "Linens are in the closet. Towels under the sink. Laundry basket tucked behind the screen room divider. Dinner is served at six p.m. in the dining room."

She rushed past him, but his grip swallowed her arm. She didn't know if she'd survive him here, living with her, a big lie hidden under her bed and in her closet, measured in size five clothing, dinosaurs, and building blocks. And her son—her rambunctious little boy who could melt hearts with his laughter—was at her parents' home in town until she figured out if and when to tell Monster they shared a son.

She was eager to speak to Alyce about the gorilla shifters being in danger. No wonder Alyce insisted that Monster stay with her, knowing they shared a son. Alyce was practically a second grandmother to Parker. "You let me go once. Don't act like you care for me any more than for a place to stay while you finish another mission."

"Dora, please. Hear me out. I have a name now. Previously suspected to have been experimented on by Mastermind years ago, Dr. Ichabod Crick, was my kidnapper and is the one responsible for mutating my DNA. I just need the EJAC to spurt out key information. A single drop is all I want. I'm so close I can taste it."

He wanted to solve his own case and hurt the person who'd hurt him and who was still hunting other shifters. It was an honorable mission as a special ops agent.

She respected Alyce, who believed in Monster. She acknowledged that she shouldn't treat either Monster or Alyce differently. Monster was a good man. A fantastic agent. Maybe, if she confirmed with Alyce that Parker was in danger, she could return to a time where both she and Monster hunted for clues. Together. They could work together. Goddess Morrigan help her. "I have rooms to attend to. I'm sure you need time to freshen up before dinner."

"I'd like that. I'd like that a lot." Monster raked his

fingers through his unruly waves of hair. "Will you be eating with me?"

She twisted free of his hold, and he let her go, but the loss of his touch struck her like a knife to her heart. She had to confirm her fears—that DIC was targeting gorilla shifters. If so, she only hoped when she told Monster about *their* child, her secret, she wouldn't break him with *her* betrayal.

A knock on the door spun Pandora around, and she left Monster standing so she could go answer it.

Mr. Duke, a bus driver for the elementary children, grades one through six, stood at the door, his hands flipping a flyer that read, *Missing Teen*. "Looks like we have a missing youngster. Keep your eyes out for the kid, won't you? Let the authorities know if you spot him. Might want to beef up security with your own son."

His tone sounded like a warning, but she parked her irritation. She wasn't angry at Mr. Duke, who'd driven both her and Monster to and from school as youngsters. She was mad at the situation; someone had potentially kidnapped a child. And she was overly sensitive; she always had been when it came to her son. She wasn't quite being honest, but she held Mr. Duke's gaze when she told him, "My security is fine. Thank you."

Pandora closed the door, brought the caption into focus, and read the details. The set of the teen's jaw was square, his dark eyes wide set. His body was still lanky, but he boasted wide shoulders, similar to how she remembered Monster's physique before he'd been turned. Now Mr. Duke was warning her about Parker's safety.

Her belly roiled, but she couldn't reject the reason Monster had returned to town. He was hunting DIC, who'd returned.

She trotted to Monster's room, entering without knocking. She wasn't stupid. The news of a son would hurt him. Honesty was a mean-ass bitch, and Pandora had formed an alliance with her for survival. But facts were facts: Monster was here. Her most precious belonging, her son, depended on her to keep him safe. Whether she wanted to admit it or not, she needed Monster.

Maybe, just maybe, when she shared her secret, he wouldn't hate her but would accept her reasoning—DIC was kidnapping gorilla shifters, and Parker was showing signs of taking after his father.

"Back to share more disappointments in me?"

She blew a breath, the timing of the conversation they needed scrambling her thoughts when she noticed the dark circles under his eyes. In her business and her life, timing mattered. "No. Disappointment in myself. Let's chat after dinner."

CHAPTER

THREE

Monster cracked his aching neck, the *pop, pop, pop* reminding him of the kettle corn that Pandora and he used to share on date nights. She had something to tell him, and he wrestled with the afternoon as it dragged on. It was just like her to make him wait, to talk to him in her own time.

He tossed and turned on the king-sized bed, his feet hanging off the end a couple of inches after he'd spent a few hours catching up on dreamless sleep and then finding his bearings.

Holy Mayan temple. He was locked up with Pandora for the night. As the smell of roasted beef, potatoes, onions, and carrots reached him, he prayed she wouldn't poison his food. It would serve him right if she did. She didn't deserve to be tortured by his presence after he'd let her go the way he had. Resentment was almost tangible in their reunion. Even if she did want to talk to him.

He planned to give Alyce an earful when he saw her at the Academy tomorrow. Facts were facts. How was he surviving the next few weeks bound up inside Pandora's Box with little relief from the agitated, yet hot little crow shifter? Her devilish champaca scent, honeyed-lilac and oranges, was driving him mad with curiosity, and he couldn't deny unrequited lust.

He was used to squeezing into tight spaces, for the record, but as big as the boxed-style home was, he felt dwarfed. Stunted instead of excited about the future and his stay with Pandora. He couldn't picture what his future looked like with DIC dancing in the wind *and* Pandora potentially in danger if DIC found out Monster was here in town and staying with her.

But his discomfort ran deeper than a DIC threat. Pandora appeared to have moved on. She didn't blush in his presence. What he'd thought at first was a positive reaction to seeing him had been nothing but raw outrage causing the peachy highlights in her cheeks to darken.

He could barely think, let alone muster the energy to show up for dinner with her scent snaking around him like the green anaconda had the last time he'd been in the South American jungle. Did Pandora expect him to sit across from her at the dining table and share pleasantries about the weather, the decor, blah, blah, blah, while she kept something from him?

"Damn you, Alyce." He cursed the woman a second time for putting them both in such an awkward position, even if, in the past, Alyce had done right by him.

Monster had a course to teach, sure, but in the background of his mind, he had a criminal to track down. His spidery senses were jumping along his spine and setting up webs to trap even minuscule information. Because that was what he needed—a break in the case of some kind. He could practically taste the closeness of key details and hard clues.

Monster sprang from the spongy mattress, strolled to the kitchen, catching Dora in the kitchen carrying a heavy pot. She didn't glance his way, but then her foot caught up on the area rug. Before he could catch her, she landed on her knees. What looked like steaming pot roast deluxe painted the kitchen flooring, so that the pot was less than half full.

"Everything is ruined," Pandora shrilled and lifted her hand, hugging one in the other. "I wish I could forget you like you have me, but I don't know what to do without you."

The shock of her admission was clear in her wide eyes and her pale face, as if she'd blurted out her thoughts before she could stop them.

Voicing her feelings kept him from responding. He pounced, his massive form landing a few inches from the woman and his feelings racing back as he cradled familiar curves, lifting her from the hot mess. Damn if he didn't still care for her at a primal level. Any caution of reconnecting with her swung right out the open window. This was his one and only chance to prove to her that, during the time he'd spent away from her, he'd never let a single day go by without thinking about her and his mistake in how he'd left her. He didn't share that he'd have to return to his mission in a few short weeks, so for now, he settled with telling her, "I'm here. It's okay. Let me see your hand. You're hurt, burned."

"I'm fine."

Just like Dora to minimize her pain. It was what she'd always done. "Let me help you."

"I don't want to need you, Monster." She pulled back from him and tucked her hand behind her. "I don't want you to bring a vengeful mentality into this house and only leave after your mission here. That isn't the kind of man I want around..."

Monster was struck silent. She was right. He would continue to cause her pain for as long as he was around.

He'd even caused her discomfort because he noted she'd made his favorite savory meal, a recipe she personally didn't particularly care for—except for the beef. In less than a few hours, she'd ended up hurt.

Dammit all to hell. He would demand Alyce find another place for him to stay.

Except the director had made it clear that no other place with a room existed locally or at the Academy. And he feared for Pandora now that he was back in town with a suspected DIC poking around.

He had to make the best of their forced proximity. As close as he was, both physically and mentally, to Pandora, it scared the shit out of him to let her down.

From his mission in South America, he'd gained a treasure trove of medical experience, including how to quickly defuse her pain and damage. He untucked her arm and inspected the wound. Her skin was pinked but not blistered. Not yet. He intended to keep her wounds as superficial as possible. "Let's run this under the cool water."

"I can take care of myself. I'll clip an aloe leaf." She pulled back halfheartedly, the tips of her fingers resting in his palm.

He met her dark gaze, a flash of intimacy captured in her eyes. "I'm not implying differently. I only want to cool down the burn so that sauce doesn't continue to harm the deeper layers of your epidermis. Then we'll smooth over some aloe vera that contains soothing glycoprotein and healing polysaccharides."

Pandora leaned into him, a tiny grin tugging at her lips. "I'm not used to anyone taking care of me."

Her admission caused a knot to form in Monster's throat. He turned on the cold water and drew her hand into the gentle spray. Her hands were soft but firmer than he remembered. She'd aged, though not in an objectionable way, just matured into a beautiful, strong, independent woman.

Who hadn't needed him.

He swiftly pushed the thought aside. This wasn't about his damn ego. This was about Pandora, the little beauty that he'd stayed true to, he realized. He wasn't one to jump girl-friends before he'd become a Lump. He and Pandora had been each other's first in all experiences that counted–their first loves, the first and only woman he'd slept with.

To his shame, he wondered if his leaving caused her to grow up too quickly, not because she wanted to but because life was hard as a shifter living within the human popula-tion. She'd been forced to move on without a partner. Not that she needed a partner, but it was nice being around those like her. Birds of a feather flocked together as they said. "Sit. I'll clean up the spill, and then I'm taking you to dinner."

"That's not necessary." She waved a dainty hand, flicking her iridescent nails. "Breakfast and dinner are included in the price of the room. And I'm not sure I want to share with you what I need to in public."

Even though she fussed, he could tell by the wince wrin-kling her forehead that she was still hurting. As far as Monster was concerned, the remaining pot roast was an ample amount to serve to guests, who could help them-selves. If they didn't understand that their host needed to tend to herself, then Monster would step in and set them straight. "I don't care about the roast or fees or the selfish needs of others right now. I care about you, Pandora."

His admission seemed to shock both of them, his pulse ramping up and her eyes widening.

"Change out of your clothes." He motioned in the direction of her bedroom, figuring she didn't want to wear the gravy that had splashed onto her apron and pant legs. "I'll take you anywhere you want to go. Price has no limit."

She held his stare momentarily. "You don't have to—"

"I do." The first day of his six-week stay had gotten off to a rough start, and he wanted—no, *needed*—to catch up and straighten the crooked image she'd formed of him. "I promise I won't talk about work."

She gave him a wry look, untied her apron, and tossed it onto the counter. She tore a stem from the aloe plant, broke it open, and rubbed the clear gel onto her hand. "You sure you don't mind cleaning up the spill?"

"I'll take care of it." It was the first time since he'd arrived that he'd caught the smile tugging at the corners of her mouth reaching her eyes.

Maybe she had forgiven him after he'd broken up with her. He'd done it so she *could* move on while keeping her safe from a distance. But he'd been a fool to believe that a love like theirs could be forgotten, and she'd said as much.

His chest constricted, his heart crushing in response to his thought. He'd never stopped loving her. The feelings he'd buried sprang to the surface like the edible indigo milk cap mushrooms he'd survived on during a rough stint in the deep tropical rainforest. He realized sustenance wasn't always food driven.

Well, duh. He'd never truly lost his feelings for her. His memories of her had kept him alive, and he wouldn't stop caring for Pandora until humans flew...

When Pandora reappeared in the kitchen, Monster lost his breath.

"Do I look okay to go for pizza?" She was wearing a black mid-thigh skirt and a garnet-colored long-sleeved top. One half of the bottom hem of her blouse was French tucked. A light sweater draped her back. A chain complimented the outfit, but the pendant was concealed.

Heat flared in all the wrong places—or right places, if hooking up was on the menu. She looked like she was ready to go dancing with those mid-calf leather boots. If he remembered correctly, Peter's Pizzeria in Willow Wisp opened up to dancing and karaoke after nine p.m., and it was close to seven o'clock now. The two of them had spent numerous nights singing "Chicken Fried" by Zac Brown Band and a slew of other feel-good songs about the good life they had in front of them.

He blew a breath, not that it cooled the steamy memories he had of the two of them entwined in a slow dance that followed their off-key singing. "You're still as beautiful as the last time I saw you. I mean that."

She smoothed her skirt before meeting his gaze. "Beauty is only skin deep. What matters is the heart. And I don't want to fight with you for the next six weeks. We have to live together, sleep in adjoining rooms, and share a bathroom, meals, everything. I'm not saying I forgive you completely, but I will admit that I understand what it's like to carry anger. It's a heavy load I've tried to leave behind. But honestly, other, more important things have left me tired, and I need to unload on you."

He wondered what trumped the B&B, but since she didn't elaborate, he let it go. It was much like he kept his quest for revenge close to the cuff. His missions had led him all over the world.

They had also led him back to Pandora.

He reminded himself not to forget the real reason why he'd returned. It wasn't only the Academy students. The urgency with which his supervisor had pulled him from the field and assigned him to work with Alyce—who'd sent him to live at the B&B—could mean only that Alyce was worried about Pandora. The reasoning had to be because DIC was on the prowl and his mentor knew information about Pandora she hadn't shared. Or one of Pandora's guests?

Monster scooped up the last of the spill, rinsed his dishcloth, and washed his hands. DIC could possibly be spying on him right now. For all he knew, it could be someone *from* the Academy or that man who'd knocked on the door earlier —the bus driver.

He swallowed his concern, his musing suddenly spinning haywire.

What he needed was a distraction that didn't include Pandora's shimmering outfit. Or his growling belly caused by his spiked metabolism, which was true of most Lumps. "Pizza? Are you sure you don't want to go somewhere fancier?"

She flashed him her palm—that burn mark had lightened to a soft rosé—and grabbed her car keys. "No. It's casual, and I'm not ready for anything more than a meal because of what we need to discuss, like I mentioned... I'll drive."

Monster watched her walk out the front door and followed along. She kept her lips sealed while she drove, him scrunched up in the passenger bucket seat, and until they entered the pizza joint. By the look of the crowds, Thursday night felt like a Friday at the pizzeria. Patrons sardined the booths, and juvenile sports team players crammed into the longer tables. Kids of all ages munched on slices of meat-topped cheese bread.

His belly rumbled at the scent of calzone and local ale.

Luckily, there was a cozy spot at the end of the bar, which Monster guided Pandora toward. He wanted to calm things down between them, as well as face the front door and oversee the patrons walking in. He'd never gotten a good look at DIC, but the man's silhouette lay plastered in his mind like the outline of one of the single slices of pepperoni swimming in the creamy-colored, melted mozzarella dotting his personal pizza, which arrived on the bar where he was seated.

Monster's face contorted, bones begging to shift, but he forced his response to his hunger back. Whether stirred by raw hunger or deep emotions, his mutated form tested him at times. He wished he was back at the Academy where he didn't have to school his features to remain human, but what did he expect? This was the human town of Willow Wisp. "You still like your pizza with extra olives?"

Her cheeks flushed as she picked at her personal pizza, mixed vegetables arranged playfully with the scattering of olive rings and sausage. "You remembered."

He knew her birthday was October 31st, Halloween, and she liked to dress up like a kid and gather candy and then eat her favorites and freeze the rest to savor throughout the year. He recalled that she liked olives on her pizza because they resembled rings, and she coveted treasures and trinkets.

Pandora, and all the secrets she held inside her heart—like her long-ago desire to become a FUC agent and work alongside her mate—still mattered to him. Even if ASS trainers specialized in her avian traits, she'd set her sights on the two of them teaming up. Pandora and Monster against the world. But she had a secret. He could tell by the way she fidgeted with the buttons on her shirt that something serious lay on her mind.

He inhaled, preparing himself for the worst, and then he spotted a tear forming in her eye. "Tell me, Pandora. I haven't changed that much. I still care about you. I'm still a good listener. I'm still trustworthy. I'd never do anything to hurt you."

"But you did." She righted her posture on the stool and swept her tears from her cheek. "You have. I won't allow you to come and go in my life. I could endure it. But I won't allow you to hurt our son."

Monster's head swam, and his teetering heart plummeted clear down to his deformed toes. If he didn't already have his elbows on the bar, he would have been flat on his face, lying in a puddle of peanut shells, shocked more than he had been the day DIC had lured him into his lair.

Her betrayal hit him hard, but so did Alyce's. He knew without asking that Director Cooper would have known. Meaning both women kept his flesh and blood from him—kept a son from him—for four long years.

He stood and beat a swath through the crowd for some fresh air, finding the parking lot jammed with vehicles, the chill of the night slapping him awake. He had a son.

Yes, he'd been expecting a tongue-lashing from Pandora.

Not an admission that she'd birthed *their* child.

While he'd been gone.

For four years.

What he'd suspected—Alyce bringing him back to teach a course and potentially question the EJAC—had been only a ruse. Alyce was smart. She'd have caught Pandora swollen with child—a shifter that could have taken after him and might now be sought out by DIC. Who knew how deep a relationship Alyce had formed with Pandora and his son?

And here he'd run once again. Had both women kept this from him believing he'd flee?

He backtracked, retaking his seat beside her, hands shaking as he clutched his icy glass. He tried to come up with a logical response that wouldn't expose his emotional state in public.

"Say something..." Pandora wiped her eyes.

Her betrayal stabbed him soul-deep, but she was as much of a protector of the innocent as he was. It was in their blood. And he'd been in no shape to father an infant when he'd first become a Lump. He was too angry, too focused on revenge. Revenge that had cost him not only Pandora but also his son. Hell, he wasn't sure if Alyce trusted him even though she'd said she had faith in him. At least she'd set him up with a second chance. That had to mean something.

A million questions raced in his mind, but one thing stood out from the others. He punched to his feet. "I want to meet him."

Pandora scooted to the edge of the stool, once again fidgeting. She drew a paper from her sweater pocket and slid it in front of him. "I don't want him getting attached to you and then you walking away. I'm sorry, but I can only agree with you seeing him from a distance."

Regret boiled in his belly. He understood her conditions. He had no idea where he'd be assigned next. But what if he found a way to capture DIC in the next few weeks? Put the mad scientist behind bars for good? Then he'd have a crack at a whole new life. A life he'd once wanted to share with Pandora.

He unfolded the paper, spotting the missing teen, the large canines cluing him in that this was another gorilla shifter—a missing shifter. "Shit."

"Exactly. Our son could be next."

Anger blazed red hot inside Monster. He clenched a fist, nearly destroying the flyer. He leaned closer, lifting her chin with his unclenched hand so she wouldn't miss the seriousness of what he had to share, even if sharing confidential information could get him fired. If they had a child, there was a fifty-fifty chance that his son would be a gorilla shifter and could thereby become a target. "DIC *is* hunting gorilla shifters," Monster confirmed. "If my son is anything like me, he's potentially in danger, and I may be the only one able to protect him. I'll need to see him. Now."

Pandora covered her *caw caw* with her hand and dug her cell out of her purse. "I have to call my mom."

"Good idea." Monster placed a tip on the table, eager to leave. He had to make sure his son was okay, and he eavesdropped on the call, using his superior shifter hearing.

"Mom, is Parker okay?"

"He's fine. He and his papa are eating banana splits. Why? Is there something wrong?"

"No. Nothing to worry about. I'll see you tomorrow, okay?" She ended the call.

Clearly, she didn't want to worry her mother any more than she already had by the evening call. Everything was normal, as far as Monster could make out. But if her fears were reality, DIC *was* hunting gorilla shifters and potentially his son. "Are you okay?"

"Not in the slightest. Monster, this is why I didn't reach out to you," she scolded. "First, you come here and get my feathers ruffled, then I'm finally calmed, and now you spring this on me?"

Instantly feeling he should comfort her, he pulled her against his chest until she glanced up at him, but still her quills pricked his hands, quivering under her blouse. "If I had known about our son, and the fact that danger could have followed me or returned to town, then I never would have come. But that's not what's happening now. No one knows that Parker is mine except for Alyce, right?"

"Well, yes, and my parents. Obviously."

Of course, she'd feel nervous and possibly distrustful of him, which left him resolved to prove to her he owed her. Owed her big for all he'd put her through, as well as wanting to make up time he'd missed with their son. "I promise you, Pandora, I'll protect both of you with my life. To do that, I have to see Parker. I must know what he looks like and vice versa. His life could depend on him trusting me."

Pandora glanced around the room, seeming to study the bartender whose back was turned toward them.

Monster waited with bated breath, hoping during her contemplation she didn't reject his offer. "I'm the only one who can protect both of you."

She turned her attention back to him, rolling the glass parmesan cheese shaker and a handful of pepper flake packs between her hands. The paper packets crackled against the faceted jar. "I agree. I will introduce you, but it's too late now. The best I can offer is a drive-by. The time together will help us get reacquainted. Regarding DIC, we need to stick together. I have a plan..."

Before he could hear her out, she tugged him from his seat, pocketing what she held in her hand. Instead of her graceful pace, in her apparent excitement, she hopped out into the night.

Paired up with his ex, meeting his son on the horizon, he just hoped he didn't screw up again.

FOUR

Pandora hissed a breath once outside the bitter night nipping at her cheeks. She fiddled with the acquired trinkets in her pocket, as if somehow they would save her son. She'd always found comfort in shiny treasures—it was a juvenile crow-shifter thing to do. But even as she'd matured and fought her klepto tendencies, when nerves threatened, she'd yet to break the cycle, fully. Some objects she kept, some she gifted. Some she attempted to track down the owner. Some she returned. But she couldn't wrap her restless emotions into a neat little package tonight. In fact, she had felt every emotion in the last hour, as if Monster held her emotions, working the beaters of her heart like she had the ingredients of their supper's stew.

It was ridiculous how she'd fussed over cutting each individual veggie for the stew, making sure that each was the perfect bite-sized piece. She'd even gone to the trouble of harvesting the vegetables from her organic section of the garden, which she reserved for her and her son.

The guests demanded physical perfection, but Pandora had always preferred quality over outer appearances. That included Monster's impeccable reputation as a top-notch special ops agent and his tentative involvement in their son's life.

Following Monster, they wove their way through the cars in the lot, a team sports van clogging her line of sight but allowing her to focus on tonight's earlier conviction.

Yes, she considered Monster and the son he'd given her her greatest treasures, and Monster's presence gave her solace of sorts.

In her heart, she knew she could trust Monster with Parker's physical well-being, but she worried about their son's attachment to the idea of having a father with an active presence in his life. *If* Parker found out the truth that Monster wasn't a man who'd stay and unite their family of three forever. "I'll need cameras, motion detectors, and beefed-up door locks put up at the B&B."

"I'll make some calls first thing in the morning. Try to secure a security company from town." The moon's glow reflected in Monster's weighted gaze as it peeked through thinning storm clouds. "I can park at your parents' and keep watch of the house."

"My parents moved to a new Willow Wisp gated community with internal patrols. If they see a strange car or person, they'll ask you to leave. The best we can do is show my pass to alert the guard we're dropping off or picking up. They're used to seeing me coming in and out. That gives us ten minutes tops to drive by and hope we spot Parker through a window so you can know what your son looks like."

"That will have to do," he grumbled and upped his pace, her compact SUV having been parked at the far end of the pizzeria lot so Monster could scout the parking area before they entered. "I don't require as much sleep as I once had.

I'll still oversee Parker's transfer from the bus to his classroom, as well as keep vigil at the B&B when I'm not teaching. If DIC is watching me, he knows I'm hanging with you, so you're a target too. I can only hope that local surveillance will expose DIC's true identity once and for all."

She was certain the furry Academy allies had access to local intel, but she tugged at her shirt collar, unease coiling around her neck. How much did Academy intelligence know about each member within the surrounding communities outside the ARSHOL facade and thereby Parker?

It pained her that she'd kept their son from his father. She had never feared for herself. However, Parker's well-being came front and center. "I'm sorry I didn't tell you about Parker. Believe me, there were hundreds of opportunities and five birthdays that you should have celebrated with us. I made the decision to keep him from you, knowing you'd understand why. You'll always choose revenge over us, and I couldn't bear losing you a second time and, in doing that, failing Parker. He's my world."

A beam of light speared into her eyes as a truck exited the parking lot, pulling onto the roadway, its engine sputtering a string of complaints and leaking exhaust.

"Don't trust anyone..." Monster gathered her hand and placed it on his chest over his heart, squeezing, until the truck's headlights vanished into the darkness. "Anyone but me. My intentions are pure, Pandora. I can't deny that you still make my pulse race like the River of the Sacred Waterfalls, Rio Upano, nestled deep in the Amazon. But I'm not the man I once was. If I had known about Parker, I would have come home to both of you."

She couldn't confirm his statement, though it was her secret hope that he would stay. Truly, she didn't understand the machinations working behind his blue-eyed gaze. She could only measure the angst wafting off his body in waves. Monster was still hunting, still ultra-focused on revenge, even more so since his son was in danger. "The proof is in the pudding, Monster. You're still hunting the person who turned you into a Lump. And getting involved with a new Lump cadet. I'm asking that you let go of the hate you cling to while watching over Parker. I don't want him to know anything but love and kindness or pick up on any kind of bad juju. I don't want him to lose his innocence. That's all I'm asking of you right now."

Monster pulled up a few lanes short of where her SUV was parked. "You can ask anything of me, Pandora. Your safety has always been my priority. But back before I left, I was a self-loathing mess who had no business in anyone's life, especially yours. I just hope you'll give me a chance to earn back your trust so I can know my son."

As a family of four exited the pizzeria and drove away, she thought about that and her plan. Of course, she trusted Monster with protecting both her *and* Parker. Certainly, Monster's loyalty to his job had never been the issue.

It was her heart that she worried about. Hers and their son's.

But their safety came first. "If you say this DIC is hunting gorilla shifters to experiment on them, then I must tell you that Parker *is* showing signs of taking after you instead of becoming a crow shifter."

"Signs?" Monster scratched his unruly hair. "Wait, he'd be four, right? That's early...Too early without a shifter elder to show him what's going to happen to him so he doesn't freak out and shut down. I've seen this with some of the rescued experiments in the FUCN'A program, and they're young adults. A four-year-old is still learning how to master spelling their name."

Pandora caught the glint of perhaps regret in Monster's glare. Regret that he hadn't been around to see how quickly Parker was growing up. It was the same look he'd shown her the day he'd broken it off with her. Then, she'd only registered the chill of his rejection. In error had she been blind to the fact that he'd cared then and he cared now?

Could she risk getting attached? Time would tell which direction Monster would go, but in the meantime, she had a potential crisis on her hands. One, she had no options but to include Monster, even if she had to ask him to keep his distance from their son.

A *crack* echoed from beside her, an acorn falling and hitting the windshield of the adjacent sedan, nicking the pane.

She sniffed back her emotions and stared into the blackened treetops, telling herself it was a naturally occurring event for trees to drop seeds. A random rodent foraging.

As natural as Parker's metamorphosis, which, sooner or later would be apparent for anyone to notice, even the predator. "I've caught Parker swinging from the dining room chandelier on more than one occasion. I don't bring attention to the shape of his brows or jaw, but both are quite prominent like yours. I'm not sure how long I'll be able to stay local…through elementary school probably, but once he hits puberty, I'll have to think about enrolling him somewhere more specific to his needs. He wants to follow in his father's footsteps."

"A special ops agent isn't as glamourous as it sounds. I'm alone most of the time and far from those who matter to me."

She held Monster's gaze. It was true, but she held her dreams close to her heart. Being an agent wasn't about her ego, it was about helping other shifters. When Parker was older, he could decide how he wanted to live his life and if he wanted to work for FUC.

That is if the evil DIC didn't kidnap her son like he had Monster, the EJAC, this new teen.

She shivered clear to her marrow. She had a dilemma she needed to quickly rectify.

Good thing both Pandora and Monster had once been a super—no, a superb team. She even felt a smile twist her lips into a hope-filled grin. "You can help me by making sure Parker gets from his bus to his homeroom class, covertly. I can't have him knowing who you are just yet."

She didn't miss the tick twisting Monster's expression as they zigzagged through the remaining cars toward her SUV. How far away had they parked?

He nodded after a beat. "I know the place. Same elementary school as we attended."

"Same bus driver—" She severed her sentence. She and Monster had shared everything.

Up until he'd been kidnapped and their lives were ruined. Then he'd made the decision for both of them to break it off. The sting of his rejection still burned, although not as much as it once had.

She needed to put the past behind them for their son and his safety. After all, she would have become an agent if she'd continued her education—a single remaining class— and accepted the position.

Alyce had even suggested it to her a time or two since Parker had started school, and she'd gained some semblance of independence. But she was a mom first, and that label filled her with tremendous pride.

Would seeing his son, and the job she'd done to raise Parker, make Monster as proud? "I only need the morning shift," she added. "I mean my parents will put him on the bus. He'll be fine riding the bus until drop-off curbside at the school."

Monster touched the small of her back and spun her to face him, deepening familiarity she hadn't forgotten they'd once shared.

"You're doing everything right, Dora, but it won't be easy for me to see my son for the first time and not be able to touch him or talk to him."

"Monster… This is about protecting Parker." She sighed, an ache budding in her throat for having to insist he forgo contacting their son. His truth both helped and harmed her. She wasn't one to let anyone else into their tiny circle.

He held up his hand. "I understand your reasoning for keeping me at a distance. But, as far as we know, DIC got lucky finding a second gorilla shifter, possibly this teen, and hasn't a clue about Parker."

"I'm not taking any chances," she said.

"I'm not asking you to. Until I know differently, I don't want you to—"

He jerked her to his side and shoved her behind him.

"*Squawk.*" Her eyes sprang wide when she spotted her vehicle. If she wasn't wearing clothing, Monster would have seen her partial shift, feathers bristling under her attire. "Oh no. Monster, someone knows what you are. That we are together, which means they could know about Parker."

Monster's icy stare accompanied a deep-set crag in his forehead. "Ooh, ooh, ahh, ahh? Written in spotted yellow banana skins? How fucking original."

She had thought her heart couldn't beat any harder, but seeing the jeer sparked a firestorm of fear. She darted her gaze around the parking lot, looking for any sign of human patrons. Then she scouted the treetops. When she found they were alone, her muscle memory from agent training took hold. She shoved off her sweater and thrust it into Monster's hands, momentarily blind to shifter rules. "I can get a better look from above the treetops."

"What are you thinking? You know it's against every law in the book to shift out in the open like this. We're bound to 'Serve, protect, and keep the humans in the dark.'"

Oh, she understood the rules, but she deemed breaking them worth the risk. Someone had possibly tossed an acorn her way, which meant she needed to search individual branches. And she'd inspect every single leaf if she had to.

"Move out of my way. DIC could be dangling from above our heads."

It was a thought that took hold. He was close. Closer than she'd ever imagined.

The sooner DIC was captured, the sooner they could all get their lives back. With little concern for her silk top, sweater, and skirt, she gritted through the pain of her swift transformation. Onyx feathers rippled down her back. She wiggled and squirmed, her clothes falling into a loose puddle on the pavement.

Monster crowded her against the car, sheltering her the best he could, and finally acquiesced to her plan. "All right. Scout the treetops. I'll search the lot and adjacent shops. We can't leave any stone unturned."

She outstretched her winged arms, and with a kick off the parking lot, she took flight. The night air ruffled her cheek feathers, the sound of those feathers like tiny pebbles against her eardrums. She hadn't considered until now that this DIC could be driven by the fact that he hated his own nature—one of a shifter.

If he *was* a shifter, he could be hiding in plain sight, as she spotted several bats darting about the night sky, nipping up mosquitoes. A family of mice trapezing the electrical wires that spanned buildings. A horned owl hooted, as if teasing Pandora that she'd been too late, too slow to change, and that the villain had already bridged a path to safety.

She paid the hoot owl no mind except to take note that the winged predator wasn't a shifter.

After a full ten minutes, Pandora landed beside Monster, retaking her form, her creamy-colored skin shimmering in the pale moonlight.

"Nothing down here. Did you see anything?" Monster pushed her skirt and top into her arms but wouldn't meet her eyes.

Even though he'd seen her nude many times, the continued sting of his rejection reminded her that she needed to keep things platonic between them. She threaded her clothes on quickly. "An owl, bats, and a family of mice. But nothing out of the ordinary."

For all she knew, the villain could be watching them from inside the pizzeria, laughing as they fumbled for answers outside, or had driven away altogether. "So now what? DIC knows you're here. Possibly. If he saw you with me, which I'm sure he did, then he'll put two and two together fast enough. Monster, Parker is your spitting image. I'm worried now more than ever that DIC's next victim will be our son."

The observation had struck her on many occasions, and a bolt of guilt had her wondering who, if anyone, had noticed Parker's rambunctious nature. If DIC was a townsperson, could he have been waiting for Parker to show signs? To mature?

Her knees shook, and a chill wormed its way to her bones.

Monster guided Pandora to the passenger side of the

car, and she slid in without a fight, even allowing him to buckle her in. If that wasn't proof of her shock, she didn't know what was. She adjusted her seatbelt and locked her side of the car, while he did the same.

When he addressed her, they were on the road. "If Parker looks like me before I was experimented on, and someone is putting it together that he's my son, it will narrow down the suspects."

Yes, she agreed Monster could decrease his suspect pool. But that wasn't what troubled her most. Why would someone want to destroy someone so perfect, so beautiful, so innocent? Monster had once been model-worthy in the looks department, similar to Parker. Even though he was a child, Parker's facial features were perfectly symmetrical, and he'd been a beautiful baby. She'd never imagined that her son would be in danger because of his attributes and genetics. "Why would a scientist target handsome, male gorilla shifters?"

Squeezed behind the wheel, Monster shrugged a single shoulder. "I have no idea, except envy, perhaps. Unfortunately, I never got a good look at Dr. Crick."

To think that the mad scientist had ruined Monster's life —no, their future—because the sick DIC slung hate at shifters like Monster was enough to spin Pandora's fear into pure anger, perking her up. She had no place in her heart for haters. She may be over her head but screw it. She was jumping on the justice bandwagon. "Now what? I'm too upset to go home."

"I'm on edge myself." Monster glanced at her. "Too bad Alyce handed me a gag order, or I'd talk to the new cadet."

Inside the Academy held answers in the form of the newest EJAC. Monster had been robbed of fifty percent of his memories with the DNA mutations. She expected a similar mental void from the new cadet. She may not have been a student for some time, or a math major, but she was certain fifty plus fifty still equaled one hundred percent. She was an accountant for her B&B after all.

Together there had to be a single clue the cadet held that would lead them in the right direction to find the monstrous DIC. That clue warranted a drive-by. *If* they could get inside the Academy unseen...

Monster might be powerful, but he didn't have wings. He couldn't climb over the wall enclosing the Academy without drawing attention from the guard, she suspected.

What they needed was a distraction, and who better to distract the guard than a kleptomaniac crow shifter with a curvy shape and a fiery personality should they get caught? She'd use her wings to fly above the landscape and scout for danger prior to infiltrating the Academy.

A zing of excitement erased any reservations she held. Parker was safe for now. But this was life or death on the line. Children were in danger, and she was just the mom to help wrestle DIC down.

To protect their son, she was willing to risk facing the wrath of Alyce, bless her soul. Better her going up against the director than Monster since she couldn't be fired or kicked out of the Academy. From here on out, she realized she and Monster were tied at the hip. Perhaps they'd always been and were destined to get DIC under wraps and find justice. "You say there's a new cadet who might have answers? Before we head over to see Parker, let's go talk to him. Together."

Monster pulled into the drive that would lead them to the Academy, a lone guard standing outside the closed gate and acting as if he were protecting the ARSHOL. There were a hundred ways sneaking into the Academy could go wrong, but Monster threw that warning out into the night. He had Pandora on his side. The two of them had teamed up to protect their son and on their first mission.

Monster looked both ways before making a U-turn. He realized this moment culminated in a 180-degree turn-around regarding his hunt for DIC. He was no longer alone in his goal. His focus had reduced from the revenge he had been four years ago to a quest to protect the innocent, including his son and the woman he'd fallen for since the first day they'd met.

He lifted his cell from his pocket and hovered a finger over Alyce's number. "As a FUC agent, I have full access to the Academy. However, Alyce informed me that the security system has some issues and I'd not yet be on the list to be allowed access. Not to mention Alyce has already warned me about questioning Willy. Technically, I have no proof that DIC left that gibe on the windshield. It could have been a student who doesn't agree with my style of teaching."

"If you're thinking of contacting Alyce, you should wait until we have evidence. You go against the woman, she could turn on you, even if I don't think she will. Initially. She adores Parker and sees you as a son. But Parker is *my* son. I went through hell bringing him into this world, a crow shifter birthing a gorilla shifter. I was a fighter then, and I'm not allowing anyone to kidnap my son. Which leaves only one option." Pandora fluffed her hair and adjusted her brassiere. "I'll do anything to protect my family."

His brows shot up in concern. She'd already taken a chance at being spotted in the community by shifting. He couldn't risk her exposing his plan to hunt DIC, which meant they had to plot out even minuscule details. He pocketed his cell. "Whoa, whoa. We need a well-thought-out plan first that doesn't include exposing your body outright on this side of designated ARSHOL. One that doesn't get the mother of my son tossed in jail."

Pandora tapped her cheek and then jabbed her hand in the direction of the back side of the Academy. "About a half-mile in, there's a sugar maple tree. If I remember right, it had a limb that extended over what is now temporary fencing, gooseberry brambles, and a steep rocky exterior in that specific spot. If the tree is still there, we can use it to breach the fence, rocks, and brambles. Possibly."

As good of a plan as any, Monster depressed the gas, taking him only a few minutes to reach the rugged back forty of the Academy. He parked, feeling the tires sink into the rain-drenched soil. The way his luck was going, he'd have to push the compact SUV out of the mud, but he'd worry about that later. At least the tree was there as described. "How do you want to do this?"

"You're the special ops agent. You tell me."

The one thing Pandora had been spared was his shifted form. He wanted to keep it that way. There was no telling which version of his mutated self would spring from his flesh when he shifted. "You stay with the car—"

"The heck I will. Parker is my concern." She hitched a breath and stiffened with resolve.

A sharp pain built behind his ribs, one he deemed as a blow to the heart rather than Peter's Pizzeria pepperoni revenge. He was still thinking about himself and his job to protect *her*, but she wasn't ignorant of the harshness of the world. "You're not going alone."

"All right. Shift. We'll both breach Fort Knox."

What if she was repulsed by the sight of him? What if, fearing for Parker, she didn't let him see their son? "I'm not pretty, Pandora. You may take one look at me and run screaming into the night, never to let me meet my son."

"Now you listen here, Monster Johnson. Shifters, if anything, have to be self-accepting. If you can't be yourself around the people who love you, then they are not your tribe. So do your thing and let me get a good look. It can't be that bad." Pandora popped open the door, tossed her clothing into the open seat, and sprouted a full set of wings, though she remained half-human, waiting for his transformation. In her claws, she held a thin tee-shirt dress.

Monster eased from the driver's seat, checking the blank darkness behind him. He grabbed his soft shorts from his pocket, something he always traveled with, and tied them to his leg with the stringed tie. He grunted until his mass took shape, animal parts sticking out of a human-sized ball of putty.

Pandora pinched a *hiss* behind her lips, but other than

that, she gave him a firm nod. "A shoebill beak is wicked on your gorilla head, and those wings are as decorative as a butterfly. And kangaroo legs, well, heck, why didn't you say so? You'll have no problem scaling that natural wall of rocks."

Monster clapped his shoe-shaped beak, the sharp horn at the tip allowing him to grip, crush, and pierce his prey, if necessary. Since he was in full shift, he didn't have the capability to speak, not with a beak for lips, and he doubted Pandora recalled her Morse code training.

With what little wings he'd sprouted as arms, he motioned to the tree. He could only hope that he'd reach the top of the rock wall with one jump and that the other side didn't have a moat filled with real alligators, though he feared betraying and disappointing Alyce more.

"On the count of three. One, two, three." Pandora took full form, once again taking to the air, her onyx feathers blending against the dark night and making her stealthy flight indistinguishable from the nightscape unless she soared under an opaque cloud.

Monster tucked his wings, placed his chin to chest, and gathered force in his big feet, using the propulsive power that originated from his flexible joints, elastic tendons, and long leg bones. He used his chicken wings for balance, much like a tightrope walker would use a pole, and hurled himself through the air, landing on top of the rocks and pricking his paw pads with a spiked tendril.

Below, a bramble of thorny gooseberry bushes stood in his way of reaching Willy Tagger.

Pandora let out a *caw* in the distance.

Barbs or not, he recoiled and propelled forward, one massive, lateral, thirty-foot hop sending him skyward until he reached the sexy little crow shifter who was trying and failing to tuck the shiny, shattered camera lens under her wing.

Monster reformed, his nakedness a spill of white leopard shapes against the dark-colored masonry building. He pulled on the pair of soft shorts.

Pandora's feathers fluttered as she retook her human form. She slipped on her dress. "Monster, you haven't lost your mojo, Lump or not. You're one impressive special ops agent."

The glass lens clattered to the ground.

"No more cameras," Pandora confirmed and kicked the lens into the thicket.

Monster chuckled and took in his surroundings. Cadets were allowed to roam around campus, shifting at all hours of the day and night. So long as they didn't draw attention to themselves, the guards wouldn't notice just two more shifters playing around. He spied the glint in Pandora's eyes.

Her excitement reminded him of when they'd been part-ners but also that he'd been responsible for the way life had morphed on both of them.

Something deep inside him told him that this was his one chance to trust her, to let her take the lead, which he'd stolen from her years prior.

Monster tucked himself into an alcove, pulling Pandora along with him. They'd gotten this far, and he wasn't taking chances of getting caught. He pushed a strand of dark hair from her eyes. "Okay. Here's the deal...Willy Tagger is bunking in the EJAC bungalows. Now that you've disabled the cameras, we don't have to worry about triggering the alarm. We *do* have to worry about surprising Willy. I haven't seen his form. He might not be as put together as I am. Or controlled."

"I'm not scared. I'm a single parent of a gorilla shifter

who's thrown temper tantrums a time or two that have busted through sheetrock." She reached over, locking her arm around his. "Let's massage some info out of this EJAC, stat."

At the sound of Pandora's determination, Monster growled, low and deep. The rumble in his throat was more than simple agreement. It was the sound of his attraction and possession of Pandora, a feeling he'd almost forgotten. It was his original self peeking out from the depths of his soul. Pandora accepted him, mutations and all. "You're still so damn hot, Dora."

"I know." She took his hand, knowing exactly where they were headed.

He murmured into the night air, "Let's get 'er done."

When Monster flanked the door to the EJAC quarters with Pandora beside him, an ear-piercing din punctuated through the door, as Willy snored inside the bunkhouse where he was stationed. Monster reached for the door, and the latch clicked. He prayed Willy didn't shift into an uncontrolled beast. "Let me go in first."

Pandora moved aside but followed closely behind him, the tips of her fingers lingering on his waistband. "Be careful."

Willy was sprawled out on the king-sized bunk the Academy had provided for young man—a special accommodation given Willy's size. His hair was a mass of ruffled brown curls that seemed damp from a recent shower. The guy's physique looked early twenties, his exposed sinuous arms and chest giving Monster access to assess the scars and deformities, much like his own—and the bond between him and Willy strengthened.

A cool hand pulled Monster around.

"Let me wake him like a mother would," Pandora whispered. "If he sees you, he's liable to freak out and explode into who knows what kind of chimera."

A visual of a saber-toothed elephant flashed in his mind. He gave Pandora an agreeable nod.

Pandora made herself half-sized by crouching near the head of Willy's bed. She reached up and placed a hand on Willy's shoulder, shaking him slightly. "Willy, I need you to wake up, sweetie."

The EJAC groaned a sleepy sound. "Five more minutes, Mom."

Pandora continued her motherly touches. "I just want to talk. Come on, Willy."

She was a natural, not surprisingly. Pandora was good at everything she did, even turning dandelion weeds that dotted her garden into a nutritious leafy salad option.

He kicked himself into gear, tearing himself away from the thoughts of her nurturing their son alone. "Willy, I need you to wake up."

The EJAC's eyes sprang wide, and he launched from the bed to the ceiling, his clawed hands more like panther pads, the inch-long nails keeping him affixed. Crumbles of plaster and paint landed on the blanket below. He blinked down at the duo as the light turned on. "Professor Johnson, what are you doing here? Who is this?"

So it looked like DIC had switched up his experiments, giving Willy feline qualities, Monster mused. "Come on down, Willy. You can trust us. We won't hurt you."

Pandora dropped her hand from the light switch. "I'm Pandora Raven. I own a B&B nearby, but at one time, I was on my way to becoming an agent, much like yourself. We have questions to ask you."

Willy studied Monster a long moment and retracted his claws. He landed on the bed and wrapped the blanket around shoulders roped with muscle. "Is this some kind of test? Did I pass? I mean I didn't completely turn, so that must mean I'm gaining control of some kind."

Monster took a defensive seat at the foot of the bed just in case Willy flashed fangs. Though Willy could strike at any moment, Monster risked getting closer, stooping to make himself less of a threat. It was what he hoped someone, or himself, would do for his son in the future if Parker were in danger and troubled—a thought outside of himself he hadn't had since his abduction. "I wish it was a test. I received a message, a taunt from someone when I was in town only an hour ago, and another teen has been kidnapped."

"Kidnapped? A threat?" Willy's voice rose two octaves. "What exactly happened? How does this involve me?"

"Someone knows I'm back in town. I suspect DIC is or will be searching for his next victim, who may include someone dear to me." Not only dear, but one of a kind and precious. Irreplaceable.

Willy tossed up his hands, spotting Monster's quivering skin. "Hey, I'm still learning what I am. I can't help you. I know nothing. I saw nothing."

Pandora scooted closer and stroked the EJAC's arm. "It's okay, Willy. We'll get to the bottom of this and find DIC sooner or later. I know this is hard for you, but you and Monster are the only ones who have been captured, experimented on, and escaped that we know of. There has to be something, some small detail that comes to mind when you think back to your abduction."

"Nothing. I told the investigators and then Director Cooper everything," he blurted out and waved his arms for a beat before he lowered them and his gaze grew unfocused.

"Something coming to you?" Monster prodded, trying to

corral his frustrations at the world. He needed answers. Answers were the only way to protect his son. What had Willy shared with Alyce? Was she keeping something from him because she'd been instructed to by the higher-ups? He needed to get into her office in WANC—the Working and Administration Networking Core—in the FUC Academy side if necessary. "Tell me. No detail is too small. It could trigger my memories, the ones I was robbed of."

Willy hugged his sheet-covered legs, rocking himself. "An engine. I remember that between when they kidnapped me and when they put me under. The authorities know that too."

An engine. Lots of cars and trucks going in and out of the Academy. Not to mention, plenty of vehicles—from cars to trucks to motorcycles and airplanes—on the location that the cadets learned to drive and operate. "Was it a low hum, like a three-cylinder winding up? A whining sound of an electric motor? A tractor's grumble?"

Willy's blanket loosened around his chest, pooling over his lap. "It was a clatter, a knocking sounding engine, *tick-tick-tick*, you know, like the shuttles here at the Academy. I think it was a diesel with a shot-up tailpipe."

Monster's belly squeezed, and the floor seemed to fall out from under his feet. He gripped the bed frame to steady himself. He recalled a loud vehicle that had left the pizzeria, but he didn't get a good look at the make and model. He never suspected DIC of driving an Academy shuttle. Could DIC be someone at the Academy? It wasn't as long of a shot as some would believe. Often the newly furry rejected themselves. Hell, Monster was a seasoned special ops agent, and he despised his form at times.

If DIC was within the walls of the Academy or even an agent, he'd know information, which was why DIC always seemed one step ahead of Monster. The man could be lurking around and driving a shuttle, which narrowed the suspects and strengthened Monster's resolve to get inside the multiple file departments across the Academy. But what rocked Monster was the fact that Alyce had refurbished a vintage 1942 Chevy flatbed truck that included a turbo diesel, one she kept garaged ninety percent of the time. "Good, that's really good. What else can you tell me?"

"Nothing right now," he chirped. "I just want to go back to sleep. I have school tomorrow. If I don't get enough rest, I could freak out. Please, I don't want to end up out of control like Daisy. After you left the school, she woke up and flipped out, literally. She busted out our white board and windows then bucked and kicked all the way to the director's office, not that it will do her much good, since Director Cooper didn't seem to have a problem with your methods to subdue her. Maybe you should talk to Alyce."

Monster had talked to Alyce until red-faced, but he could tell by the twitch of her lips that she was holding back key information. Mind you, he wanted to believe she was innocent, but something whispered in his ear, telling him needed to stay guarded. "Alyce used that chloroform trick on me on my first day. It proved to me that everyone runs on self-preservation. Every day as an EJAC is a test. A test of conviction and resolve to turn the hate you feel for DIC into something good. You want to be a hero someday?"

"Nah, I'm not the hero type. Not exactly. I just want to be left alone. Mostly." Willy twisted his mangled hand in his lap.

Monster's heart fell a few notches. He knew all too well how the cadet felt. It was a coping mechanism to trauma, flight, or fight. Doing nothing was as good as running, in

Monster's opinion. "I see potential in you, and that isn't isolation."

Pandora put her hand on Monster's leg and split her gaze between the two men. "I think we should go speak to Alyce and let her know about the banana message, or whatever you call it. There may be other reports that we don't know about. Willy, are you sure you don't want to join us?"

Willy burst upright, drawing the blanket with him. "I don't want to get involved, especially with Alyce. I'm nothing but an experiment who can't control his shift. If I get caught snooping around the interior offices, the whole Academy will be talking about me spazzing out instead of Daisy."

Pandora stood and placed herself between the two men. "Willy, you are exactly who you're supposed to be. Now let's put our heads together and come up with another way to investigate this engine noise before we go off on a tangent. Like, did you hear the motor start up or shut down? Depending on your distance from the engine, it could sound different."

Willy leaned forward, grabbed a notebook and a pen off the desk, and handed it to Pandora, since his fingers were twisted into odd angles that made working a pencil challenging.

Monster sat, brushing her shoulder with his, as if he could somehow, through metamorphosis, show her his memories of a hand around his mouth, a white towel with chloroform pressed to his lips. His legs had banged against metal as he'd been dragged, one row after another, until he felt his body squeezed between two partitions, where he'd been cuffed. He now believed he had been transported on some kind of multi-seater vehicle. Perhaps a shuttle? Or the back of a truck bed. The vision failed to fully form.

Up until now, he hadn't remembered anything more than being taken out with a chloroform-laden handkerchief. Which just happened to be how he'd subdued Daisy and how Alyce had taken him down. He motioned to Pandora. "Write diesel engine times two. I recall it as well."

"Oh, and a smell," Willy interjected, lifting a finger. "Alfalfa and sweet grasses, maybe root vegetables. It's weird that Direct Cooper gnaws on carrots, and she drives that Frankenstein truck…"

Monster braced himself as a wave of awareness struck him a second time. Alyce was *Monster's* mentor and stand-in mother figure. Never would he have imagined Alyce in any other role than steering him in the direction of the truth. But before Monster realized, he stood over Pandora and drew her to standing. "I think we have a problem here in town and at the Academy. With Alyce."

"Like what? The two are mutually exclusive," Pandora defended.

"Are they? Alyce is into everyone's business. She does have a thing for raw veggies as of late. She has connections all over the world, and it wouldn't be the first time a higher-up was found involved in some kind of conspiracy." A false animal rescue charity scandal came to mind as he ushered Pandora outside, leaving Willy to retire. He guided Pandora toward the open landscape that led to where her vehicle was parked.

Pandora held up near the rock outcropping, under the broken camera. "This is worse than I've imagined. But we have to be careful. You can't rush in and break into Alyce's office or interrogate the woman without a good reason and without hard facts and legitimate evidence. She's been a blessing to both of us. Believe me."

Monster let his thoughts flow past his lips. "I feel it in

my gut that this perp has ties with young shifters. Believe me, I don't want it to be Alyce, but she knows the workings of the community outside the walls of FUC, as well as the FUCN'A as the director. This woman who knows my internal thoughts and workings, who I've trusted since I was turned, has kept from me the existence of my own child. My son, Dora. If she can look me in the eyes and tell me that you've moved on and are doing well without even a blink, what other kinds of appalling acts is she keeping from us? What kind of games is she playing and has she played us all along?"

CHAPTER

SIX

Pandora bit the paper with the notes she'd written out of Willy's notebook along with her dress as she took flight, transferring both to her claws when she was airborne. She scoped the blanketed landscaping, keeping a lookout all the way back to the SUV, but she mentally wrestled with the facts: If Monster was right about DIC's true identity, her dreams to return to the Academy and her son's apprenticeship there could be doomed. Which meant what? How would she protect her son without Alyce's connections short and long-term—the backing of the director and the FUCN'A? It didn't matter that either of her worries were in the future, she craved order, and Alyce had provided that for Pandora.

Monster's arrival had turned her world upside down with worry, and clearly chaos.

Even though the meeting with Willy had gone off without a hitch, Monster was stuck in his shifter form after he'd bounded over the bramble of barbed bushes and boulders and landed opposite the ARSHOL side of the fence.

She'd witnessed him angry before. Betrayal was an evil parasite that was almost impossible to truly shake.

Monster lunged skyward, landing with a *thud* and leaving a crisscross of eight-foot-long roo prints in the rain-soaked soil.

She tossed the note into the car and then jerked her dress on quickly, anger making her belly fill with what felt like nests of devil's grass. If they got caught, it would open up an entire garden of wiggly worms, which meant she needed to pull out her nurturing persona and calm Monster down. No way was she letting a missing chink in their plans taking over. "Come on, Monster. You can do this. I know you feel betrayed by Alyce, and angry, but until we have solid proof, there's nothing we can do but be vigilant with Parker."

He just quivered as if he were in horrible pain, grunts and clenched roars of discomfort spewing from his massive jaw—at least he bore the resemblance to a gorilla under his foot-long beak and snow-leopard skin. That fact that he had control over his shape let her know that he was still inside the mutation, even if DIC set out to erase the man she'd loved. "You're still you. The man I fell for. Come out, Monster. We can get through this and come up with a plan of attack."

Snap. Crackle. Pop.

Truly, she felt like Monster might spontaneously combust as he fought with his internal beast. "Don't let this newest glitch get the best of you. It's hard facts we need. Not speculation."

His feet retracted, and his kangaroo legs buckled. He fell onto all fours, sweat pouring off his forehead. For a flash, his body held on to his true gorilla form, one she'd fallen for what seemed like lifetimes ago.

"I'm back," he growled. "Let's head to the B&B. I can hack into the ICBC to check the vehicle database and see how many diesels are operable within the area—to see if Alyce has access to any of the Academy shuttles—other than her personal vehicle—and whatever else I can find on the crack-the-whip camelid."

She approached Monster, handing him the clothes he'd shed earlier, helping him as if he'd reanimated to his Willy-aged self when he'd been kidnapped. In her heart, she didn't believe that Alyce was their nemesis, but she skated on ice sheets. "Monster?"

"Yeah." He slid on his pants, hiking them over his hips, and tossed his shorts into the car.

"It's okay to regroup and take a step back to process this lead. It could be nothing more than our minds desperately wanting answers and making something out of nothing. Do you really want to charge into the Academy and accuse Alyce of being DIC?" She hand-ironed her dress hem, nerves teasing her to grapple with the seriousness of the potential situation.

He scrubbed his face with a hand, perhaps pondering, as she was doing behind her serious gaze. She planned to keep her thoughts undercover, but still they spun circles in her mind. Alyce had made a deal with her, but had what should have been a barter between friends come with a secret agenda instead? The offer to take Parker under Alyce's wings when he became an adult had seemed convenient, friendly, and done with love. But had it been contrived? Good goddess Acanthus, was Pandora setting herself up to align with Monster's thinking? Was Alyce DIC?

No. No, Pandora wouldn't feed into her worry until she had evidence. After she calmed things down with Monster. "Maybe sleeping on it is a good idea."

"If I can find sleep." Monster banged the butt of his hand onto the block wall.

She approached him, careful to measure if his body was anywhere near morphing. When he met her gaze, she drew him to her. "These tasks seem mountainous, but we will get through this together."

He folded into her, his head tucked into the crook of her neck. "I never thought I'd find you again. Not like this. Not helping me after what I put you through."

She stroked the back of his head, swaying slightly as she attempted to calm the beast. He was protecting her then as much as now. It had taken her time and reconnecting with him to see that the good in Monster hadn't been erased by his zany, altered genetics. "It's okay. You're safe with me. And I know I'm safe with you."

He raised his head, his dark eyes an indigo blue under the night sky. "You've always had my back, Pandora. Always putting your needs aside to take care of others, but I plan on changing that and helping you. I'll earn your forgiveness. I'll stick around. I won't leave again. I'll be here for you and Parker. If I have to leave FUC—a place I once called home—I will. You are important to me, you and Parker. I won't let anything stand in the way of us. Not even the woman I've looked to as my mentor and friend."

A tear threatened to reveal her fears. As nice as that sounded, she wasn't stupid. Monster was an amazing agent, and FUC needed him. Perhaps it needed *them*, she pondered. And there would always be the threat of this DIC or a DIC copycat. But maybe she could accept that the best defense against gorilla hunters was the two of them teamed up. She sandwiched his cheeks with her hands and drew him down, pressing her lips to his.

Monster deepened the kiss. He wrapped his hands

under her thighs, lifting her so she wrapped her legs around his waist. "I never thought I'd kiss you again."

She'd had the same thought and bridged the gap once again. Lip-to-lip, she ignored the songs of crickets and katydids and far-a-way murmurs from cadets ignorant to the two of them hooking up at the edge of FUC. Their kiss dampened her acute senses so all she felt was him. His caresses stoked her inner flames. Her heart, the one she'd guarded for so long, the one she'd laced with chains and padlocks, melted as if he'd never hurt her, not even once. This was her person, her one and only true love, and denying him wasn't part of *her* DNA. "If something so untenable is happening..."

She didn't dare finish her sentence, because it would mean allowing Monster to finish his last mission, both of them finally getting what they truly wanted. She, her family back, and Monster, his revenge. "Then I'm willing to give you time to find DIC, even if that means working alongside you. Even if, goddess forbid, DIC turned out to *be* Alyce."

Monster spun her around and then pressed her back against the side of the car.

His lips were velvet, the swoop of his tongue dancing with hers in a sensual salsa of its own. Hunger purred from his throat, igniting a fire in her core.

"Tell me to stop and I will."

Her common sense battled within, telling her to hold back, telling her that she shouldn't let herself be wooed by a man she barely knew after their time apart. But her heart, her body... They wanted Monster inside her, filling her with his seed, his monstrous chimera DNA be damned.

They were a couple and belonged together in the most primal way. Together, they needed to reconnect, to sync their hearts and their minds. Fuse trust and fortify the fortresses of their souls. It was the only way to face their uncertain future without regret.

She shimmed up her dress faster than Monster removed his pants. His glorious shaft filled her to bursting as he kissed her neck, plucking at the skin with his teeth.

The inferno inside her turned molten, and she swiveled her hips, bucking into him until the glossy sheen of his shoulders caught the starlight, until she was begging him to go deeper, faster, harder. If she'd missed anything about Monster, it was his sheer will to please her beyond pleasing himself.

He tossed her upward, placing her on the roof of the car.

She yipped and then giggled at the thrill and chill of metal against her thighs. Then he buried his mouth against her sensitive parts, his magical tongue working her clit until it blossomed and the stars above danced behind her eyes.

It was then, only then, that she forgot the reason they'd parked behind the Academy, forgot the pain that had lain crooked between them, forgot that she was a mom who'd set her needs aside years ago, forgot that she'd yet to utter words of forgiveness. It was her and Monster, together at last. "Don't stop. Please, never stop."

Her orgasm skyrocketed her mind to a bliss-filled ecstasy, one she'd only ever shared with Monster, as if the planets had fallen away and then realigned at their joining. She shuddered in his arms, her shrieks of pleasure causing her toes to curl, as if she were in crow form and clinging to a branch for dear life in the middle of a blizzard. A storm he was sheltering her from.

"Let it out, beauty. I'm right here." Monster lowered her from the roof.

A distant horn blared, the echo fading into the darkness.

The scare of being caught only upped her intentions to

see him satisfied. She braced her hands on his shoulders, her core still pulsing with pleasure. She wasn't about to let him go unfinished, even if they were loving one another behind the ARSHOL.

She took his girth in her hand and guided it to her core. She wrapped her legs around his hips, using her heels for leverage as she ratcheted her body up and down. The pressure teased a second orgasm from her, but she bit back her joy. This was about Monster. She wouldn't verbally admit that she'd never stopped loving him. Not yet. But with her body she caressed every spasm that rippled through his manhood, squeezing her inner muscles to knead every last drop he could fill her with.

Call her reckless. Stupid. Insane or mad with lust. This was Monster Johnson, and he'd always been her FUC man.

"Pandora, you feel so damn good. So fucking amazing..." He clenched his teeth and tilted his head back, exposing the corded muscles of his throat as he groaned through his release.

When Monster was spent, he leaned her against the car and roamed his hands over the voluptuous crests and narrow valleys of her body. "Well, that wasn't how I saw our first time together after so long playing out, beauty."

She'd always loved his moniker for her, and she smiled up at him, tears of happiness filling her eyes. "Are you saying you were anticipating me sharing my bed with you?" she teased, as if offended. "Why, Monster, I'm not that easy."

"You've never been easy, Pandora. Just too perfect for someone as damaged as myself."

"You're not damaged, Monster. You're new and very much improved. You've grown since we broke up. I can see wisdom behind your eyes."

"Wisdom," he scoffed. "We just had sex without a condom. That's stupid."

"Reckless of both of us. But I doubt they make condoms your size."

He pulled her dress in place and the sweater back around her shoulders, buttoning the cashmere piece, but not before planting a soft kiss at the top of her breast. "I wouldn't know. I haven't been with another woman since I suspect we created Parker, which was before I was kidnapped."

She blushed, pride filling her, not only for Monster's confession but for her own acknowledgment that she'd never had another man after she'd taken Monster. "I was a fool to not go after you."

"As if I'd allowed anyone in my space." Monster blew a long breath. "All I had room for was revenge."

As gingerly as possible, she asked, "And now?"

"All I want is you. You and Parker. Tell me how to get both of you back, and I'll do it."

She treaded lightly. Sex had a way of clouding the seriousness of what they'd discovered inside the Academy. Nothing had been resolved, but maybe she could admit that she was no longer scared of a future with him. "We have to settle a few things first. Like, what about Alyce? Do you really think she's involved?"

Monster shook his head and pulled up his pants just as two distant beams of light from an approaching security car shone their way.

Her pulse sped. "This could go badly."

He ushered her to the passenger side of the car, jammed his body into the driver's seat, then, without turning on the headlights, engaged the engine and headed in the opposite direction of the oncoming patrol car. "I think our sexcapade may have attracted attention from the guard."

"Oh, just a few animal sounds from under the full moon. A snow-leopard-kangaroo-shoebill and a crow shifter." She laughed, and it was the best sound she'd heard coming out of her mouth in a while. "Head toward my parents' house. You need to see Parker."

"Really?"

"Yes. Really."

Monster depressed the gas, propelling them all the way around the back of the Academy to the side road that led into Willow Wisp. When he entered the main street, he flicked the headlights back on. "Tonight, you made me feel like myself again. It was nice."

"It was." In fact, it was one of the most thrilling and self-gratifying endeavors she'd had in years. He must have felt a connection. He gathered her hand, brought it to his mouth, peppering soft kisses on the back of her hand and pinning her with a look that reminded her how much she'd loved him.

"I think we should stick together while working this case."

A small smile played on her lips. She searched for any sign of insincerity. But all she saw was genuine remorse and a desire to move forward. She took a deep breath and nodded as they approached the manned entrance to her parents' home in the gated community. She slowed only enough for the security scanner to read her card. "To protect Parker, I'm willing to give it a try. Take a left and then the next right. It's the corner house."

Sure enough, Parker shone through the window. He was sleeping in a recliner and wearing his favorite pajamas, the ones with the playful, red-cape-wearing monkey stamped all over them, which she'd purchased online. "There he is."

Monster depressed the brake, and his eyes began to leak. "He's beautiful. Damn, Pandora, what have I done? What have I missed?"

Four years with your son traded for vengeance... "What happened is in the past. You have a way to make things right with him, but I have to remind you that he's an innocent little boy who believes his father is saving the world in far-off lands. I just don't know how he'll react to meeting you if you come out of left field. He's going to be shocked and have questions. He's going to demand time from you that you don't have. You're here for six weeks, but then what? Put yourself in Parker's position," Pandora cautioned.

Monster scrubbed his chin. "You mean he has a picture of a hero, and I might let him down if DIC somehow gets to him or I fail him."

Her heart nearly shriveled at the thought of DIC stealing Parker's innocence like he had Monster's, Willy's, and now this other teen. "Yes."

Her mother stood from the sofa, gathered up a sleeping Parker, and strolled to the back of the house.

Monster followed the movement with his stare. "Your mom is as nurturing as you are."

"I'm not sure about that. It's after midnight, and Parker wasn't sleeping in his bed, but then my parents love to spoil him, and I don't have the luxury of enforcing boundaries because they're my only option, and they love him dearly. I'm picking my battles. As long as he's happy and safe, he can fall asleep watching television."

Monster continued to stare at the empty window and swiped at his cheeks. "It's late. I have a busy day tomorrow tracking down a security company for the B&B, a class to teach, and I have surveillance at my son's school."

As proud as Monster sounded, and as much as she didn't want their time to end, she had responsibilities at the B&B. "I'll call around for security since I have local contacts. I have breakfast to prepare for the guests. After the way I left dinner, there's bound to be some complaints."

"We both have jobs to see done. I'll oversee Parker in the morning and keep my distance from him until you introduce us." Monster leaned over, kissed her forehead, gave her a firm hug, and then popped open the door and trotted into the night, his body disappearing into the lush landscaping that surrounded the house.

Her heart swelled again with Monster's dedication to protecting their son. In much the way in camouflaged himself, she trusted that he'd find a way to blend in with the slush of parents who walked their children to the bus stop fronting the gates in the morning. Now, it was her turn to protect Monster. She retrieved her cell phone, found the last incoming number, and hit the green handset icon.

"Pandora, is something wrong?" Alyce's voice cracked from sleep.

She could picture the woman wearing a fancy nightgown and her hair bound up in a bonnet. But was something wrong? She and Monster had broken into the Academy. They'd suspected Alyce of being DIC. They'd crossed Alyce's orders to leave the young EJAC alone. But that wasn't quite her concern. "You tell me. Monster and I went to Willow Wisp for dinner. When we came out of the pizzeria, there was a message written in bananas on my windshield. Monster and I scouted the area, but we didn't see anyone."

Sheets rustled through the receiver. "It's after midnight. Why didn't you call me immediately?"

"Because something tells me you know more than you're letting on. Now I'm wondering if this *agreement* that you've made with me about Parker gaining easy access into the Academy when he's of age isn't a way to get to him, to single him out because he's a gorilla shifter."

Alyce chuffed. "Are you accusing me of being some mastermind behind the kidnappings? To that sweet little boy? He's like my grandson, and I treat him as such. What's going on, Pandora?"

She'd pussyfooted around long enough. She was Parker's protector. If anything, she needed the truth and hoped that her keen senses would pick up any hint of a lie from Alyce. So far, the woman's defense seemed logical, but who could Pandora trust? Someone was stalking gorilla shifters. "You wanting Parker doesn't make sense to me when he's yet to show signs of shifting. For all I know, he may never come into his nature. Or he could follow my lineage as a crow shifter and choose another path other than becoming a FUC agent."

"Would that be so bad?" Material rustled again from the receiver. "Listen, Pandora. I warned you about Monster's mindset. I suspected he'd overreact when he learned of Parker's existence. He's hypersensitive and hellbent on finding the one who harmed him. I thought four years would settle him somehow. But with the new threat of Dr. Crick potentially in the area, I'm worried."

"So you're saying you know nothing about any other messages or kidnappings?"

"I'm afraid not. I'm innocent of any wrongdoing or withholding. I want nothing but happiness for you and for Monster. He's like a son to me, and Parker is a joy."

Pandora didn't know what or who to believe. What did she expect from Alyce? If Alyce was innocent, Pandora had practically labeled her villainous. If Alyce was secretly DIC, Pandora had basically alerted the woman that she and Monster were on to her. Russell Crowe, help her to make the right choices. "That may be true, but I'm not sure who I can trust. My mind is spinning."

"Listen, Pandora. I didn't realize how accommodating Monster's supervisor would affect him. I'm sorry that I put you in the middle. My offer is still good, Parker coming here when he reaches adulthood. But I'm worried about Monster and his mental capacities. He may not have been as ready to return as I expected. I'll have him stay at the Academy somewhere. It's what he wanted originally. There he can undergo psychological testing to determine his stability."

Caught off guard, she let out a *squawk*. Monster hadn't exactly changed his mind about staying with her. But had he plotted to love her and leave her? Now that he'd had his way with her, was he no closer to joining her in her home than he had been any other night during the last four-plus years?

She shook her head, feeling a sense of whiplash, doubting Alyce and Monster who both seem to be pitted against one another. But she decided to stick to her convictions and go on the facts, setting herself up to investigate this new information.

"I can tell you're shocked." Alyce sighed. "I'm truly sorry. I'm not sure the note on the windshield wasn't Monster's way of playing into *your* fears. Playing with your past and evoking feelings as your and Parker's protector against some phantom evil he's engrossed in finding."

She would have argued, but in fact, Monster *had* rushed outside. He'd had ample time to arrange a few bananas, strange as it was. Perhaps Monster was mentally damaged, more than she'd ever accepted. Could she trust him around her son? Should she wait until she could prove his mental stability? She considered if she was flirting with disaster regarding all of their futures. *Fact, Pandora, Facts.* "I'm sorry I woke you. It's best we start fresh in the morning..."

She ended the call, exited the passenger side of the car, settled into the driver's seat, readjusted the seat and mirrors, and drove out of the community toward the B&B. She wasn't sure who she could trust, confused as she was and overly suspicious of everyone. Until she gathered hard facts, she doubted she'd sleep tonight.

CHAPTER

SEVEN

Monster startled from the distant rooster's crow, the sound alerting the agent that his time watching Parker was over for the night. But he'd promised Pandora he'd bridge the gap between when her parents put Parker on the bus to when he'd arrive at school, promptly at 7:55 a.m. via the school district transportation. The school grounds were off-limits to those who weren't registered as parents or guardians, but in Monster's opinion, the parking lot was fair game for men like DIC.

Monster stood and shook off the stiffness that had settled into his bones after his seven-hour shift stuffed into a bush. He hand-pressed his attire and trotted to the street fronting the home, noticing activity inside.

More than anything he wanted to catch a better look at his son, but Pandora's mother escorted the youngster to her awaiting van that would take him to the bus stop fronting the gated community. Enough morning walkers strolled past, and cars whizzed by to allow him to blend into the hustle of the morning rush. He was a master of camouflage even in broad daylight. He tossed on a jovial grin and a leisurely stroll, making him appear like another resident taking a walk before work. As he passed the house he guarded all night, he heard Pandora's mother and his son's conversation as they made their way to their van.

"I won't have you arrive late again," she scolded the child. "We don't have time for donuts. You should have eaten your granola, strawberries, and banana."

Monster clenched his hands, feeling the injustice in his core. His son had to learn that nutrition was important, but still Monster felt like the child had been unduly punished by being withheld breakfast. Not that Monster could do anything about it. But he planned on discussing the injustice with Pandora.

He glanced both ways at the street that fronted the curb. When the coast was clear, he wove his way toward the neighborhood entrance, joining in the parents and children who darted past the guard station.

If DIC was anything like him, he'd find access to Parker easily, a condition that forced Monster to decide he'd keep watch over Parker the following evening. But what about the next night and thereafter? He didn't require as much sleep as a human or normal shifter, but he'd have to close his eyes at some point.

His cell buzzed against his leg, and he lifted the device, spotting an incoming call from Alyce. Followed by a text: *Call me back. We need to talk about your sleeping arrangements.*

Monster picked up his pace. The last thing he needed was Alyce switching things up on him or giving him shit about what he did with his free time. Not until he had answers.

The second call he let fall silent in his pocket. He wouldn't let his son down.

He jogged down the main road, thankful the sunrise had

yet to fully make its appearance. Dressed in jeans, shirt, and jacket, it wasn't like he could pull off jogging for exercise. When he arrived at the school, he kept to the outskirts, waiting for the bus that would no doubt appear in the next half-hour, which gave him time to ring Pandora.

He raised the cell, using the B&B card Alyce had handed him to place a call. When his call rolled over to her voice-mail, he figured she was busy with her breakfast responsibilities and left a message: "Hey, beauty. I'm at Parker's school. Smooth sailing last night. Talk soon."

He thought about filling the pause with words of adoration, appreciation, and joy, but he ended the call. He was consumed with the possibility of Alyce's deception. Why would she become involved in altering shifter genetics, specifically gorilla shifters? Was it to advance her career by molding a chimera shifter into a special ops agent who required little sleep and held three times the strength as the strongest natural shifter? Or was it to stir up problems, as if the llama shifter hated *her* nature and those like her? The more he considered the reasons, the blinder he became to the truth.

The rumble of a motor rattled Monster from his ruminations, and he glanced at his watch. Just on time, the elementary school bus rolled into the circular driveway and parked, the sound of the brakes letting out a harsh *hisss*.

Monster's heart beat out of his chest when he spotted Parker.

The youngster bounded from the school bus. He wore a carefree smile and backpack, the straps waving about his thighs. He was a mixture of the two, that was for certain. Anyone who knew Pandora and Monster would recognize the boy as their child.

"Good-looking boy..." The bus driver stacked hands on

her chest. "But then all these youngsters are my pride and joy. You know how it is, as a parent. Which one is yours? Oh, let me guess. Master Parker. He has your eyes. But by your expression and the fact that he trotted past you, I take it you're not in the picture."

Pain hammered Monster's sternum. He'd been AWOL in more than just Pandora's life. But he'd made a promise to Pandora, which he wouldn't break. This woman had no business in Monster's personal life, other than assuring Parker got to and from school safely. Still, he felt defensive. "Of course, I'm in the picture. He's a little boy who's more interested in his friends than his dad."

That seemed to appease the woman, who scurried back into the bus and engaged the engine, exhaust fumes hanging in the dank air as it idled.

Monster kept back a few feet, scouting the parking lot and incoming students and parents. Sniffing the air for any recognizable scent that would further trigger his memories of DIC. As it were, few parents seemed to be as concerned about their elementary-aged child being kidnapped since the average age of abductees was twenty. Still, Monster kept his eyes and ears glued to anyone who seemed out of place loitering in the parking lot.

"Look out."

The ball came out of nowhere, bopping Monster in the back of the head. It was partially deflated, looking like a dodgeball, red and textured. He retrieved the ball and sought out the youngster who'd kicked it his way.

Parker held out his hands. "That's my ball, mister."

Monster knelt to the kid's eye level. Parker was taller than his classmates. He had Monster's blue eyes and jawline but Pandora's cheeks and nose. Every fiber in Monster's body told him to pick up the child and hold him close, to share the secret Monster held. Promise Parker his father would never leave him again and that he was home for good. "This ball here?"

"That's mine."

Monster spun the ball around on the tip of his index finger. "How do I know for sure?"

"It's my teacher's. Class number is right there." He jabbed a finger at the number scrawled across it. "If I don't return it, I'll miss out on recess."

Monster took in Parker's scrunched brows, instantly noting the kid understood that returning the ball was important. The right thing to do. He handed it back. "Well, I wouldn't wish any trouble on you. Now, hurry back. Class is about to start."

As Parker burst into a sprint, Monster wished he'd told the kid not to talk to strangers, no matter how nice they seemed. But what left him reeling was the cape made from one of Monster's shirts that he'd left behind, waving in the wind, urging Monster not to ruin Parker's impression of his father.

A tear perched on his lashes just as a familiar hand landed on his shoulder. When he faced Alyce, he figured it would go one of two ways. Alyce had spoken with Pandora, and Pandora had sent Alyce his way, or Alyce had found out about Willy and their little meet-up last night. Either way, he needed to get into Alyce's files and learn more about the EJAC. Considering he didn't have his truck with him and needed a ride to the Academy, Alyce showing up at the school seemed like a win-win. "I was just going to call you back."

"Were you now..."

"That's right."

"Good. Because we need to talk. Right fucking now,"

Alyce spit and jabbed her finger at his chin level before guiding him toward her ride and practically dragging him away from the kids and prying human ears.

Monster caught the discerning gaze of the bus driver he'd spoken with earlier. Seemed everyone was suspicious of him when they should have been watching their backs and keeping watch over the children with near hawk-eyed precision. "Move along. Nothing to see here."

Monster wasn't particularly trustful of getting in a vehicle with Alyce. Especially Frankenstein, as Willy had named it. Not after the director had drugged him, once upon a time, like Monster had drugged Daisy. But his feet kept in time to Alyce's pronking gait, her stiff legs sending her a foot off the ground. Before he could refuse, they were on their way back to the Academy, giving him ample time to have a hard-earned conversation with Alyce.

"Put your seatbelt on before I lose it." Alyce revved the engine and set them on their path toward the Academy.

Monster recognized the good-cop, bad-cop routine, even though Alyce was a director. She was a tough leader, full of pride over her graduating cadets, and knew how to play the interrogation game. She also had cared deeply for him. She had taught Monster everything he knew, which had allowed him to graduate with honors and obtain his current title. But as an agent, he had to ask tough questions. "Before you have the floor, where were you last night? Spend any time wandering the Willow Wisp pizzeria parking lot?"

Alyce gripped Monster's arm with a free hand in a way his mother had often done. Damn her for triggering memories of his mom.

"You're fucking kidding me about this note, right? You

think I left it?" She spat and tightened her grip, pushing the speed limit. "That I'm somehow working with DIC?"

Did he? He wasn't ready to accuse Alyce, but the woman knew everything. Of course, she would. She conversed with Monster's higher-ups and with Miranda, who knew everything. Which only fueled Monster's suspicions. Plus, Willy had divulged that he had shared key intel with Alyce. Why was the director of FUCN'A nose-deep in special ops missions? "I'm not sure what I believe. It seems damn convenient that I'm transferred home to work with Willy and there's another kidnapping."

Unless Alyce was setting him up... To take the fall.

"You're not a scapegoat, Monster. You're my last hope in finding justice for one of my cadets. I don't want Willy to suffer as you have. I want him to find forgiveness instead of letting his hate rule him. I don't want him missing out on a future."

As Monster had done. Traded family and happiness for hate and revenge. He sat quietly, the engine rumbling under his feet. Could have been half an hour before he spoke. "I have an obligation—"

"Not the way you've gone about it so far. I warned you to stay on the down-low. To focus on your students. To stay away from Willy. Now he's threatened to disenroll from the Academy. According to him, you interrogated him last night. You and Pandora. What the hell were you thinking? I warned you not to engage the EJAC. He's not only fragile minded, but he's also dangerous."

Disenrolled? It was exactly what Monster had done before Alyce tracked him down. Before Alyce saved him from himself by getting Monster the help he needed. Maybe Monster *had* gone too far. After another ten miles, the ARSHOL came into view. Damn place was in the middle of nowhere. Just how he felt now. Lost. Looking for answers. No doubt Willy was as lost. "I'll go after him."

"You'll do no such thing. I've sent a staff member and contacted his parents. They'll convince him to return. In the meantime, I'm concerned about you. You've been obedient and a pleasure to work with. But you've been here twenty-four hours and you're already causing a ruckus, lying, disobeying orders, getting members outside of the FUC community involved in Academy business." She drove through the FUC entrance.

"You mean Pandora."

"Hell yes, I mean Dora. She's not an agent. She doesn't get to involve herself in investigations of this magnitude. Now, not only is she snooping around but she has the opinion that I'm some kind of madwoman with an agenda to steal her son. Your son. Which is so fucking far from the truth. I love that little boy like he's my own grandson."

He didn't know what to believe because Alyce had never let on that she had a relationship with *his* son. "What's going to happen to me?"

Alyce parked and exited the truck, slamming the door with a *crack*.

Monster followed. "You didn't answer my question."

Alyce paused under one of the large elms. "You're pushing my buttons, and I'm trying not to say the wrong thing. But at a minimum, you're having a psych test after class. Then I'll decide—"

A crow touched down between them, and Pandora took her human form, arms outstretched between the two. She tossed on the dress she carried and pulled Alyce to talk privately, but Monster's acute hearing picked up the conversation.

"I know you are worried about Monster and what state

he's in." Pandora gave Monster her back and lowered her voice even more. "I didn't get a wink of sleep last night thinking about everything you said and every second I've spent with Monster since he's been back. And you're wrong about him, Alyce. You have to be, because I couldn't love him if you weren't."

The words melted him, his heart feeling like a gooey hot fudge sundae. Pandora loved him. She was standing up in his defense against Alyce. Still, Monster didn't like her involvement if doing so put her in danger. Monster took their pause in conversation to butt in. "Pandora, I don't want you involved."

"It's too late for that, but I understand you want to protect me. Monster, if our son is in danger, then we need FUC backing to work on leads." She pegged Alyce with a pleading glare. "Both Willy and Monster recalled a bus of some kind. A diesel. Now there are school buses and transport vehicles here at the Academy. There are personal vehicles, those like yours, and farm equipment. All we are asking is that you contact the investigative team leader to look into as many avenues as possible."

"A team has been on this case since before Monster was kidnapped. We've scouted the area and have investigated all types of transportation, both within the local towns and here. We've found no leads," Alyce offered, punching fists at her sides to back her knowledge.

Monster stepped forward. "Maybe it's time for a new set of eyes. Fresh eyes. If all we have to go on is a motor and some structural elements, that's not much. Now there is this banana and maybe some DNA on the stem. If I knew every detail, I could give the case a crack."

Alyce shook her head, wisps of black hair framing her face. "I'd say you're both crazy, but I know that's not the truth. I'll see if another agent or two can be pulled back into the case, since it involves my cadets. But until I have concrete evidence of any kind of internal involvement, the two of you are to return to your positions. You as a mother and businesswoman. Monster, your students are waiting. For the time being, teach them to do the opposite of what you've done in the last twelve hours."

Monster didn't press about the psych test. He nodded, resisting a jaded salute. "On it."

When Alyce climbed back into her suped-up truck and drove away, Monster took Pandora into his arms and forced any irritation he held for her to take a walk, even if his anger had appeared briefly. She was protecting their son. She and Alyce had an agreement. Whatever future moves Monster made, he needed to make them without Dora. If Monster was in DIC's sightline, he'd have noted Pandora close behind. Something Monster had to avoid if possible. "Alyce is right. I overreacted. Now that I know of Parker, I'm on high alert."

"I'm just happy I got here in time to ward off any irrevocable repercussions."

"That's not your responsibility." In fact, once the words hit him, he had to follow through. "I don't need you helping me on this case or any others. Your job is raising Parker. I don't want to take time away from him when he only has one parent."

Pandora took a wobbly step. "What are you saying? You don't want to be involved in our lives? In your son's life?"

No. He wanted to be with his family more than anything, but both Pandora and Parker were in danger if he was in the picture. Look what had happened to Willy. One meeting with Monster and Willy had fled. Now *he* was in danger, as was the public should he shift. "It's the last thing

I want, but it's unsafe around me. I won't put you in danger."

Pandora's eyes glistened. "But I'm falling for you. I want us to be a family."

Seeing her emotions gutted him. But this was life or death. Her life. Their child's life. And their deaths. If DIC was out there, Monster would never rest.

Angst burned through his veins, his anxiety making him twitch. His heart wanted Pandora and a relationship with his son. But his mind was locked on his truth. He wasn't a man to love. He was a Lump. A monster. A life alone was his destiny. "Go home, Pandora. Forget about me."

She kicked out her hip and raised her head high. "I want to call you an even bigger asshole than the last time you turned your back on us."

He left her standing in the parking lot, hating himself more than the first time he'd left her because he cared. He cared about her. About her and Parker. He wasn't a selfish asshole, as he'd been four years ago or as she'd labeled him. He wasn't wrapped up in his own pain. He was completely aware of how he was hurting her. But to protect her, he had to put one foot in front of the other, even though he was the one breaking from heartache this time around.

"Monster."

At the sound of Pandora's cry, closer than he anticipated, he spun to face her.

She threw her arms around his waist, hugging him to her naked body. "I said I *want* to call you an A-hole, but you're not. Not for a second. I know what it's like to be alone. I know why you're pushing me away. But it won't work. Not this time. I'm sorry that I called you a bad name. That was the old angry me coming out. Only, I'm not that woman. I want to hang DIC by his balls as much as you do.

Which is why I'm coming to your Coping class with you. It's us against DIC, and Alyce may be on the fence about trusting your sanity and intentions, but I'm not. You are a good man. Sharp-minded. Selfless. We need to work together for our son. What do you say?"

Caught off guard, Monster staggered backward, crossing into the line of traffic—

A horn blared and brakes squealed as a VW Bus came to a jerking halt, the scent of burned matches and rotten eggs wafting from the exhaust.

"*Squawk.*" Pandora flapped her arms, startled.

"Watch where you're going." Monster slammed his palm on the front grill. "Didn't you read the five miles per hour sign? You could have killed us at your speed."

The passenger door flew open, and Willy jumped out, a mess of brown curls flailing from under his ball cap. He jogged toward Monster with an apologetic look skewing his facial features. "I'm sorry. I got scared. But it's scarier outside these walls than here with you. If you'll have me, I'd like to re-enroll and join your class. After seeing you shift last night, I've decided to be a badass like you, able to hop a wall in a single bound."

Pandora flanked Monster's side. "Glad to hear it. We were just heading over to the class."

Monster appreciated Pandora taking over. It gave him time to process all that had happened in the past few minutes, but there was still vital missing information. Nothing had really changed. He didn't know for certain if Alyce was involved or not. Hell, even Willy drove a diesel bus. What he needed was intel. "Wait a minute. We still need to see those files."

Pandora gasped. "You can't be serious. Monster, Alyce

gave us all a second chance. Don't expect her to give you a pass this time around."

Monster's intuition pushed him to investigate the files. He wasn't sure where Alyce had driven off to, but she was no longer on the premises. Time was ticking. "Why don't the two of you go on without me? I don't want either of you getting in trouble should I get caught. Not that I'm planning to. I'll be in and out. Then we'll meet up in class."

Pandora grabbed Willy's hand first and Monster's second. "We're in this together. I'm trusting you and your intuition. Show us the way... We'll watch your six."

With Alyce gone, he believed in his gut it was now or never. "Follow me."

CHAPTER

EIGHT

Pandora checked the wall clock as they neared the Academy file room adjacent to Alyce Cooper's empty chamber. They had five minutes to grab the necessary files, anything on Willy, which Monster was certain was inside Alyce's office, and Monster's FUCN'A file, and get to class. And she still needed to borrow clothes. "I think we should divide and conquer."

"I agree. I'll take Alyce's office; you and Willy try to sneak past the file clerk. Grab my file, but don't waste time going through it. I'll peel out the info later." Monster jingled keys he must have pick-pocketed while driving with Alyce and opened her door. He reached around the corner and tossed her a lab coat. "You'll appear more official wearing this. Been hanging in here for eons with a few others. I don't think she'll miss it."

She wasn't self-conscious about her body. She was a shifter, and going braless or nudity was part of the game. But she felt more comfortable covered by a second layer in Willy's presence. Plus, it would be hard to seem official, if she needed to partially shift with her rump pillar held high. "Okay, Willy, I guess you're with me."

The click of the door shutting Monster inside Alyce's office was just the kick she needed. But when it came down to dragging Willy into their shenanigans, she spun around to face the young man. "I believe the best way we can work as a team is if we split up. You can better serve us by acting normal, which means getting to class on time. If we're late, we need you to tell the class you ran into your instructor who mentioned he'd be five minutes late at the latest."

"I'd rather be here. It's my life that was ruined. If there is even a chance at finding this DIC, I want to be the one to shake some answers out of him." Willy's face flushed, and his eyes wobbled in their sockets.

If he shifted right here, no telling how much danger they all could be in. "Calm down. It's okay. We'll make sure you're the first to know if we find out anything remotely important."

The tremors shaking his body settled. "Yeah, okay. I'll see you in eight minutes."

Good thing the kid had been clocking time. She still had to get past the gatekeeper.

She followed the corridor and turned right. The sign above the entrance told her she was in the right place. Still, she approached cautiously, peeking around the corner. Measuring if anyone other than students mingled in the corridor.

One young woman sat at the desk, head down and reading over some papers.

There was no way Pandora was walking to the file section unnoticed. Which meant she needed a distraction. She trotted back to where she came from in search of Willy, but he was nowhere in sight. She thought of grabbing Monster, but he only had minutes to clear Alyce's office, a precious moment she decided she couldn't steal from him. She was, after all, the one to suggest they split up.

She strolled back toward the file clerk, took a deep breath, and prayed for a miracle. "Excuse me, I'd like to check out a file."

"You have a note from your supervisor?" The woman ran her gaze up and down Pandora's facial features.

Think quickly. "I am a supervisor."

"Or really? I haven't seen you here before."

What would Monster do? She stiffened and righted her knee-length coat. "I was called in by Alyce Cooper. The director. If I don't have the file to her in the next two minutes, you'll have to deal with her."

The woman poised a pencil over a sheet of lined paper and grumbled. "Name?"

That was a good question. Pandora couldn't exactly give her real name since she was no longer an active member of the Academy. She wasn't about to rat herself out so easily. What she needed was a miracle or a murder of crows to run as a distraction. But she was the only crow shifter in view. She felt inside the coat pockets and found them empty. Shoot.

Sweat threatened to out her nervousness. "It's here somewhere..."

"I need proof before I let you in. Otherwise, I'll be calling security."

She checked the inside flap. Bingo.

Relief flooded her. Until she glanced at the photo, pinching her lips to hold back a *caw* of disapproval. She definitely didn't resemble the white-haired woman with thick-rimmed glasses. But what were her choices? She handed the tag over to the woman, hoping the clerk didn't spot her shaking hands. "Professor Stealth, yes, that's me."

"You don't look like that bald eagle shifter." The woman squinted.

The bald eagle shifter in the photo had short, white hair. "The salon works miracles these days. My eyes are brown instead of gold due to colored contacts in lieu of glasses."

"You have a second form of ID?"

Sure, Pandora could rattle off her FUCN'A ID, but then she'd be caught in a flat-out lie as a dropout cadet. "Number is there on the card. You can check me out while I find the file I need... Or speak to Alyce directly if I don't deliver."

The woman slid her glasses down the slope of her nose just as a member of the clerical staff requested her help. "Wait here."

Pandora had only a moment to think and shifted into her true form, which had never let her down.

With a shudder and shake, the dress and lab coat pooled on the ground at the foot of the half wall. She picked up her dress, and hopped up over the desk, landing on the right side of the space. She took flight, making sure to navigate between the rows of files and keeping lower than the shortest shelving unit.

On her way to the Js—J for Johnson—she passed the Rs— R for Raven. She spotted the file clerk with a folder in her hand. Pandora perched on the edge of the shelf until the woman strolled away.

When it was safe, Pandora shook out her human form, gritting past the discomfort, until she stood naked once again. She pulled on her dress as a thought struck her. Maybe she was here to see her own file. A glimpse at what her life could have been. She dashed to the Rs and found her file quickly. The file wasn't softened from use like she suspected Monster's might be but crisp and new—and thin.

She opened the file, spreading out the handful of pages across the floor to give the illusion that she'd mattered as a potential agent. As a woman before she'd become a mom. How had she somehow lost her identity and dreams along the way? How had her life narrowed to four thin sheets of dried wood pulp?

She slipped the file back into place, cursing her curiosity, but then paused. These were her files. Proof that she'd been on her way to graduate as an agent, if only she'd completed a final course in conflict resolution. Her urge to confiscate them grew strong, but she didn't have a place to hide her papers, even though that never stopped her from holding on to a souvenir before. But for now, she glanced at her unfinished transcript and placed it back in the file, promising herself she'd see her career through someday, then headed toward her task, fighting back her emotions.

It didn't take her but five seconds to retrieve Monster's file.

It weighed as much as a watermelon, sheets sticking out at odd angles, supporting proof of his importance in the world. Importance that DIC had tried to steal from her man.

Her heart continued to hammer in her throat for fear she'd be caught. She had no business rummaging through Monster's personal files. The task was to grab it and go.

But as much as Monster craved the truth about himself, she yearned for information too. To paint a picture of the life he'd had without her. To somehow paint herself into his backdrop, however minuscule.

Risking getting caught, her curiosity got the best of her. She ran her fingers down each page, swiftly at first, and then leisurely, realizing that most of the newer pages had most likely been collected by Alyce and stored within the folder. He was, after all, Alyce's golden student. His accolades were as impressive as the cases he'd solved. There were photos of him with other agents. Of him and Alyce in what seemed like the deep tropical forest and surrounded by indigenous people.

Monster had even made the world news in what seemed like an animal cruelty case that spanned continents. But Pandora knew all too well that these animal look-alikes were shifters. Monster had cracked a case that had gained global attention.

While she'd what? Raised their child. Poured her heart and soul into the B&B to keep her and her son financially stable. Sometimes barely feeling alive in Willow Wisp.

She shouldn't have felt slighted that Monster had succeeded without her. But deep down, perhaps she needed to give voice to her feelings. She felt betrayed by Monster. Not all the images had been taken after he'd become a chimera. He'd excelled as a cadet, FUC agent, and in a world she'd never felt like she belonged.

They were supposed to be a team.

Partners for life.

DIC had stolen what she'd held most precious at the time.

Now, DIC was back and threatening their son.

Maybe she and Monster weren't meant to be. Maybe she was being selfish for even considering that they could be a family when he obviously craved more—as the photos detailed.

A tear slipped free, but she brushed it away. She wasn't the self-serving kind. She was a mom, and moms didn't have time to think about their needs when their child's livelihood was at stake. This was just her darkest fears rising. She mattered. She mattered to Parker, her precious little boy.

The truth was she needed to skim the file and leave it, as there was no sneaking out a folder of this magnitude. Her past dreams were as dead as Monster's gorilla-shifter-self finding its way home or identifying and serving justice to DIC.

She flipped another page—

Her fingers froze.

Young men lay strapped to a row of beds.

One boy was receiving an injection, the agony twisting his face into a combination of pain, fear, and rage.

The sight twisted her stomach, and she covered her silent scream.

Monster held the syringe.

Monster held the boy down, a child that was not more than five years older than Parker.

As if she could be struck down herself by the visual injection, her knees buckled and she fell to the floor, taking the file with her. These photos must have been collected by rescuing agents at some point and made their way into his file. "Monster, what have you done? Who are you?"

She peered closer, using her crow eyesight to focus on the name written on the badge hanging from the lanyard around his neck.

The pedestal she'd placed Monster on cracked and crumbled. Her lip quivered and her emotions raged war, anger and betrayal socking her belly. Tears added to her betrayal, her own body giving away to her pain. "Dr. Ichabod Crick."

"I never wanted you to see that."

The heat from Monster's body as he crouched beside her

nearly singed her skin. Which would have mattered if she wasn't numb from head to toe. She opened her mouth, attempting to force her nest of thoughts into a string of intelligible words, but all that came out was a croak of disbelief. Disbelief that Monster *was* DIC. That he was using her to get to Parker. Who was this man? This monster?

"Look at me."

She couldn't pull away from glaring at the multiple photos sprawled around her.

Monster with other men, but her focus lay on him. Only him.

The betrayal and this twist of knowledge stabbed her in the heart, a crushing pain trading places with the newfound joy she'd felt for him only hours ago. Even though her mind begged her to see past the photos, to make sense of what she was looking at, even that the photos could be photoshopped from the real DIC, she uttered, "This can't be true. Tell me you didn't experiment on children. That you had no part in Willy's mutations."

Monster draped his hands at his sides. "I'm missing time, Pandora. I don't know what I was forced to do. I'm not DIC. The coat and name tag I'm wearing there are as much mine as the coat you wore and tag you flashed not ten minutes ago. You have to believe me. This is a fabrication. Someone is trying to frame me."

She gaped at the revelation that Monster had missed time. He didn't know what he'd done, and she had only one person in the world that she had to protect. Her son. *From* Monster. "I can't believe I let you near Parker. What if something triggers you... To hurt our child."

"I've never once lost control in my Lump form since I escaped. I'm clear-headed. DIC didn't steal my mind he only controlled it while I was under his influence, most likely using some kind of mind-altering drug. I'd never hurt our son, Beauty."

She jabbed her index finger at the picture. "But you're hurting others. It's right here in living color."

"Come on, we can talk this out. It's why I needed my file. I don't want these photos getting into the wrong hands and being used against me down the line. So far, I've managed to convince my supervisor, Miranda, and Alyce that these photos are staged. I've worked in the field for five years, successfully. Not a single issue. I wouldn't have been allowed to work or teach if I wasn't clean. But since I've returned, something's up. Can't you see? It's someone higher up. Pandora, you have to believe me. I'd never intentionally hurt anyone, especially a child. We still have a mystery to solve. Come with me. We'll do this together. I believe in us. I want to be a family with you—you and our son."

The relationship between them was dead. So was her trust in Alyce because she hadn't been straight or upfront with her and the dangers associated with housing Monster. Even if there was the slightest chance Monster could be persuaded, she should have been informed. Monster had strung her along in an attempt to cover his tracks. Possibly using her as an accomplice. As a partner in identifying and delivering their own child to a psycho. She didn't trust a soul. She needed to fly, and now. "I don't know who or what to believe. I need time. Time to process the truth."

"I'm telling you the truth. I'm not DIC. He must have used me while I was under his spell. Hell, I can't remember half of my time there, which is why I've sacrificed my life to find him, to make it so he can't frame another shifter for his monstrosities."

The clock on the wall read 11:00 a.m.

Thirty minutes before she had to arrive and ready herself to pick up Parker from school. It was the excuse she needed to part ways. To think. To either reject or come to terms that Monster was a monster.

She sprouted wings. Her lips reformed to a hard keratin. Her dress pooled around her claws, and she gripped hold. She pushed off the ground, tucked her feet under her tail, and darted back from where she'd come, zigzagging over the desk.

Pandora didn't bother grabbing the lab coat on her way out as she thought of her next move. She'd remove Parker from school. She couldn't even hide at her parents' home because Monster knew the location. No, the two would disappear. It was the only way to protect Parker from DIC.

Pandora pumped her wings faster than she ever had, making it home before anyone could follow her in a vehicle. She returned to her human form and slipped into her dress, for fear she'd startle her house guests if they saw her in the garden with nothing on but her birthday suit. She grabbed a lightweight grocery bag, packing only a day's worth of clothing for herself. Knowing her car could be traced, she forwent driving. She called for a taxi to meet her at the school. She hadn't forgotten about a locksmith or security, but she no longer needed that service, not where she was headed.

She returned to the garden and shook out her shifter form, taking to the skies and leaving her dress on the pea gravel. In broad daylight, she hovered close to the tree canopies that dotted the small town, the plastic bag swinging from her talons. Finding the perfect spot to dress without being seen, she landed at the tree line that skirted the school grounds. She dressed in jeans and a T-shirt, slip-on shoes. It was the best she could do for now. And all she'd been able to carry.

An end-of-day announcement sounded over the intercom.

Pandora sprinted into action, mingling with the incoming parents who were picking up their Just B4 pre-kindergartners. She waited at the half-gate, eager to find her son. As soon as he was let out, she'd usher him into the taxi. She had enough savings to rent a car in the next town over and "surprise" Parker with an early birthday present at a theme park or zoo. Something he'd enjoy that would give her time to process her way to hide them.

"Excuse me, Ms. Raven?"

At the sound of Parker's principal's voice, Principal Epona, Pandora spun around to face the woman who'd been overseeing the staff and students at all grade levels since Pandora and Monster attended school. "Hi, Ms. Epona. How are you?"

"Tootsie. Call me Tootsie." The woman clicked her tongue and adjusted her scarf. "I'm well. I just wanted to compliment you. Parker is such an amazing child. He's scored the top of his class on state entry exams, and I'm just waiting for the official paperwork to present him with an accommodation and entrance into the GCABC program for gifted children."

Pandora's belly fluttered, and her chest warmed. Parker was smart. Well beyond his classmates. That wasn't a secret. It also made him desirable, in her opinion, should he catch DIC's attention. "He's a special child, but I'm not sure if the Gifted Children's Association of BC is right for him. He's only five."

"Mmm..." Tootsie showcased a tight smile.

Pandora didn't react to Tootsie's condescending look. It

was as if the woman thought she could do a better job than Pandora in making a choice for Parker and raising him, which was absurd. It was hard to imagine anyone loving her child more than she could and making smart choices for his future. "Well, thank you for telling me about his testing."

Tootsie stepped closer, touching Pandora's hand. "If you don't mind me intruding, Parker reminds me of his father. Too much not to notice that he and Mr. Johnson were playing ball earlier today. It's so important for boys to have a father figure in their lives. Will he be staying with you at the B&B? It's a lovely respite. I hope Parker can spend time with me at the equine rescue. We have lots of incoming needing grooming and attention."

Sure, everyone in Willow Wisp knew of Tootsies sanctuary. From the street, the animals could be seen in the pasture grazing. But Pandora was still stuck on the fact that Monster had interacted with Parker when she'd specifically asked him to wait. Had Monster made plans with her son? Plans that didn't include her? Plans to somehow drag him into the underworld of experimented-upon shifters?

She shuddered clear down to her recessed tail feathers. She had to be wrong, but still she questioned, "Were they together long? Did you overhear their conversation? I haven't yet told Parker his father is in town. It's a surprise I'd like to keep between you and me. Until the right time, when I've introduced them properly."

The woman's face paled, and then her cheeks flushed. "I see. But I have to warn you, Parker is intuitive. He's already shared with the class during share-time today that his father is coming home tonight to be with him. He was quite excited and nearly bounced off the walls like a playful chimpanzee."

Pandora clenched her teeth around a gasp. Her son was

no more a chimpanzee than Monster. They were gorilla shifters, both formidable in their sizes—deep chests and brutish facial features. They were both gorgeous in her eyes. "Yes, Parker is an excitable young boy."

"Not usually. He's very serious at times, almost broody. But today, I saw him light up like fireworks. He's so much like his father in that both of them connected at an emotional level. I even witnessed Mr. Johnson wiping tears from his eyes. You have a very special man in Parker's life. I hope the two of you can parent in a way that benefits Parker." Tootsie patted Pandora on the arm and strolled in the direction of another parent.

Pandora felt as if the tension she carried had exploded, tearing apart the fibers of her being.

What was happening? Was she making a mistake by leaving town? Was she seen as somehow stifling Parker's growth? As if she didn't know her own son? If Monster *was* DIC, he'd have had an opportunity to nab Parker. But he hadn't. According to the principal, he'd acted as any father who'd met his son for the first time—showcasing an emotional reunion for the world to see. Bringing out the best in Parker, when, perhaps, Pandora had not.

What was she doing? Running.

Leaving behind what she'd always wanted—a family of her own that included Monster.

They'd been wrong about Alyce. Alyce wasn't DIC. She had been Pandora's lifeline helping her understand Monster and was an involved member in Parker's life.

Monster may have worn that DIC nametag, but back when he'd first been kidnapped, he was no more a geneticist than she had been. She had to come to terms that he'd been in survival mode. In a life-or-death situation, sometimes you had to do things that weren't pleasant.

The school bus blared its horn.

Pandora jumped, almost tripping over her two feet. She'd been tripping up all day, but she was resolved to make things work on the home front. She didn't spot the taxi, but she'd paid upfront so she didn't worry about wasting his time when she popped her head through his open window and sent him back on his way.

Although her mind still wrestled with the lack of information she knew about DIC, in her heart she knew Monster wasn't him. No matter what the photo showed. He was no more DIC than she had been Professor Sandra Stealth, the bald eagle shifter.

The school bell rang, and Parker jetted from his classroom, spotting her right away, a wide grin on his adorable face.

For Parker, she was better off *with* Monster than without. She needed to be proud of what Monster had accomplished. He'd sacrificed in much the same way as she had. She loved him and accepted him as he was. No two individuals had the same path, but she and Monster had a common goal, which was to protect the innocent, and that was something to be proud of.

"Mommy, what's in the bag?" Parker peered inside.

Nothing but air and rash plans. "I thought we'd walk to Mamaw and Pop's. It's a beautiful day. Would you like that?"

"We might find some treasures, like shiny rocks and acorns." Parker skipped alongside her.

Under the sunny afternoon day, she took up Parker's hand, guiding him along the safe edge of the roadway, and headed toward her parents' house. The fresh air and exercise cleared her head and allowed her time to think up an apology to Monster. To do that, she needed privacy from innocent ears.

A rumble sounded behind her, and the *hisss* of brakes caused her to turn around as an empty school bus rolled up beside her.

The door folded open, and Mr. Duke, the school bus driver, leaned forward on the gear shift. "Why don't the two of you hop inside? The older grades are on a field trip, and I only had one child to drop off, which I've done. I do have time to take the two of you to the far side of town and your parents' community..."

Thankful for the break, Pandora directed Parker in front of her and climbed inside. Mr. Duke wasn't the pre-kindergarten driver, but she'd known him since she'd attended school. Plus, her heels and arches were throbbing in her flat-soled shoes, and she'd ditched her cell phone at home for fear of being tracked. Silly her. "It's farther than I realized. Thank you so much."

He spread a crooked smile across his face. "No. Thank you."

Huh? She met Mr. Duke's gaze, dark eyes, and the tall ears that suddenly sprouted from his human head. She had only a moment to piece together what was about to happen. "Parker, run."

Too late. Mr. Duke bucked from his seat and wrapped a cloth around her mouth, shoving her to the ground and ignoring Parker's pleas to get off his mommy. "You made capturing the boy nearly effortless."

Pandora squirmed, wrenching her head from the toxic fumes plastered to the material. She kicked until tunnel vision threatened to take hold.

A pendant swung from the man's neck.

She'd found a match at her B&B. OMG. Could the

woman who had stayed in her home have been the perfect accomplice? Or the actual DIC in disguise? A way to gather intel about her son?

Mr. Duke pulled out a gun from under the seat, letting her see he was armed.

The last thing Pandora heard from the driver was a muffled echo. "Welcome aboard, Parker. Ichabod has been waiting for you…"

NINE

Monster hustled to his class, finding the students waiting for him in the outside grassy area, but his mind was a million miles away and eternally stuck on Pandora's well-being. He'd hurt her again. How was he getting her back when she believed he was DIC? Which was one-hundred percent untrue. It had to be. Otherwise, he'd remember something so horrific, wouldn't he?

He didn't belong teaching a coping class when he hadn't come to terms with his own nature though. It was him that criticized and hated himself, clearly giving Pandora the motivation she needed to flee. She didn't want his anger rubbing off on their son.

He punched one fist into the other, growing frustrated at his outer rage and the shifting of his bone structure that slid and popped under his skin.

Students covered their mouths, clearly fearing him.

Which they should. He was barely holding on to his control after letting Pandora down. He'd been living and attempting to satisfy his ego and for revenge for too damn long, which was no way to live. Alyce would agree with his thinking there.

Monster didn't know how to change and channel all the hate he carried toward DIC, the bastard, and likewise himself. That darkness had spilled over onto Pandora, and he'd stained her with his sordid past.

But the dislike he felt for himself was just a flicker compared to the inferno of repulsion he'd seen behind Pandora's gaze. She hadn't believed him when he'd told her he wasn't DIC. Why would she? He'd done nothing but lie to everyone around him, even Alyce. His mother was probably rolling around in her grave over how he'd dishonored her good friend. But the anguish he felt most was how he'd disappointed Pandora by not sharing the full scope of what DIC had done to him—that portion he could remember and evidence collected by agents—and what the mad scientist had forced Monster to do to others.

Damn. The distance between him and Pandora was a dagger to his atriums, the chambers seeming filled with acid that choked him up and caused a painful lump to sprout in his throat. But perhaps she was better far away from him. He could feel something building, as if DIC or his accomplices were close—or at least closer than they had ever been.

A breeze pushed a swath of cottonwood flurries across the open space, and Daisy covered her mouth with two hands, holding back a teary-eyed response to the allergen as her knees begged to buckle.

Monster hadn't only returned to the Academy for an opportunity to teach a class. That was his way in. He'd heard whispers from other agents that DIC had the ability to scan incoming shifter students. Naturally, Monster had made the jump that the person was involved in the FUC Academy.

Of course, he'd harbored suspicions about Alyce. Alyce had been the puppet-master to just about everyone at some point in their furry journeys inside the Academy. She'd certainly guided Monster. She had an arrangement with Pandora. Possibly regarding Parker.

But if Alyce was innocent, then who and where was DIC? Clearly, he was in plain sight and keeping an eye on Monster. "Willy, you're up."

The gangly EJAC took his place in the center of the grassy knoll and ditched his ball cap. "I don't know... What if I hurt someone?"

Monster had been in complete control when he'd found Pandora skimming his file. He'd hurt her, the part of her that really mattered—her heart. In his experience, getting hurt and causing pain was a shifter condition. Perhaps a human condition. Hurting someone wasn't always through a physical connection of fists.

Either way, life was a sacrifice. He just wished he'd traded places with Pandora and had let her check out Alyce's office instead of his personnel file. Alyce was squeaky clean. So was Willy, as far as his file was concerned. The kid didn't know much, as he'd mentioned. If Monster had listened to his intuition instead of looking for where to place blame, he'd have come to that conclusion sooner.

He'd been a fool and look where that had gotten him. Nowhere.

He wasn't ignorant to the fact that Pandora was curious. The crow shifter was no more in control of stealing a peek at sensitive information than Willy was in control of his topsy-turvy shifting abilities.

Yes, Monster's control hadn't been the answer to keeping Pandora from getting hurt. He sure hoped he could remedy the damage. Because DIC was still out there… "Cadet, I'm here for you. Let it all out. Everyone else, give Willy some room."

Willy met Monster's gaze, his downcast look one of defeat and fear. "But what if no one wants me around after they see me? What if I'm not liked? Shamed? Expelled?"

Monster was hit by a fact. Pandora had accepted his physical appearance. She'd said as much. He needed to find her and pray that she'd see the truth and accept what was inside of him and the love he had for her. Pandora was his person. Willy needed to find his peeps beyond him and Pandora. "Then they're not your people. But let's worry about that later. This is your day to shine. And you will."

The kid palmed his hips. "It's hard to focus with Daisy on the brink of shifting. I don't want her attacking me while I'm having an out-of-body experience. She's an ass when she gets upset."

"I'm an ass?" Daisy shot back. "You were nothing but a lowland swamp critter before you were *improved*."

Improved? Monster delivered Daisy a warning glare that he wouldn't tolerate any kind of prejudice. For all he knew, that was what had tripped up DIC initially and guided his abominable plot to use gorilla shifters as test subjects. "That's enough from both of you. Donkey shifter and gorilla shifter differences ended the minute you two decided to enter FUCN'A."

"Ugh." Daisy groaned and rolled her eyes. "Let's see what you got, Lump."

Monster patted the air. He didn't want another grievance served, and there was only one way to keep these newbies from verbally complaining. "New rule: we're shifting together."

Daisy shot Monster an irritated glare. "Are you drugging all of us this time?"

He'd apologize to the student after class. He owed her that. "Not this time. I want to see what I'm working with. Don't hold back. On the count of three—"

"Stop." Alyce trotted over, waving her hands.

Monster's pulse ramped up as Alyce's plum-brown lips twisted, as if she were fighting shifting herself. For as long as Monster had known his mentor, the woman rarely got riled, unless there was some kind of threat. Unless Alyce had caught Monster red-handed, as in she knew Monster had breached her private office or something. But Monster had been careful. He'd sported gloves and glided around the office as silent as a ghost. "What's wrong?"

"You tell me. First, you're in my office. With a cadet and a civilian—"

"Pandora—"

"Is an adult woman who knows right from wrong. Or at least she was of sound mind before you came into the picture and turned her against me and the Academy." Alyce shook her finger and her head morphed slightly, her llama lips sputtering spittle.

To say Alyce was spitting mad was an understatement. "Listen, I can explain."

By now the students had formed a semi-circle around the two, their muffled conversations spiking concerns.

"The time for explanations is over." Alyce pranced a circle around Monster, as if her legs were springs. "I trusted you, and you broke my trust. I don't want that kind of betrayal showcased for the students to see."

"It's too late for that," Monster mumbled under his breath.

Daisy sneezed, shifting midair, and the donkey shifter kicked Willy in the backside.

Willy's arms flailed as he caught air. His legs turned into thick, leathery-skinned stumps, propelling him skyward a good four feet off the ground and delivering him on top of Daisy's cross-striped back.

"*Hee-haw, hee-haw.*" Daisy's donkey legs became coils, attempting to eject the EJAC.

Willy's eyes transformed to deep-brown marbles, and his facial bone structure turned his human-looking nose into a slender muzzle. "*Oh eeeeeeee.*"

"Stop it right now." Alyce chased after the two newbies, her pencil skirt riding up her calves.

Daisy kicked up her legs and swung her head, baring her chicklet teeth as she tried to remove the mid-shifting Willy off her back by tearing at his strained athletic jogging pants.

"Do something, Monster. Don't just stand there gawking," Alyce ordered.

Willy didn't last four seconds before he tumbled off, taking a hoof to the solar plexus. "*Click-click-cooook-URRRRRR.*"

Nothing but the disgruntled sounds of Lump-Willy shot through the air, but Monster was certain it was a cry for help and jumped into action.

Monster dove after the cadet, getting pummeled with Willy's three-foot-long antlers from the scimitar horned-oryx —an IUCN Red-listed mammal that was extinct in the wild— that had sprouted on the EJAC's white-rhino body. Head-locked by Monster's arm, Willy dragged Monster a good thirty yards before the Lump shook free of the special ops agent.

DIC had clearly had access to some kind of zoo that specialized in North African mammals, allowing Willy to morph between feline and ungulate species. Which rubbed Monster the wrong way since his missions had clearly taken him to a somewhat erroneous continent. His efforts could have been applied closer to home. He felt strung along by the higher-ups. He groaned and huffed a string of curses.

Alyce was on the phone, several of her security members having been alerted.

Monster sprinted after Willy, but the wild-eyed chimera made a quarter-turn, dropped his head, pawed at the ground, and barreled straight for the few students who hadn't shifted. "Look out."

A hand on Monster's arm spun him around.

"You're fired." Alyce shook her fist. "Get out of my sight before I have you brought before the Furry Alliance Court."

Daisy brayed and galloped toward Monster, a ruby pendant necklace constricting her windpipe but catching the midafternoon sunlight. Ears pinned, she opened her mouth, snapping teeth as she tore into Monster's T-shirt, taking a chunk out of his shoulder and sending him backward.

The necklace had some kind of paralytic attribute when he saw it, as if he'd been sent into a trance by a staged hypnotist. It triggered a rush of memories that spun him in circles as he chased after each one. The gem also tempered the pain from the quick-healing wound, as if erasing his feelings, even those deep feelings he carried for Pandora. The rush of knowledge about the laboratory and what DIC looked like combined with his numbness. DIC was middle-aged with a slim build, and all male, a donkey shifter himself. But that image combined with his shock, a numbness gloving him. It caused Monster to pitch left and fall with an ear-piercing *boom*.

Spine aching from landing on an embedded sprinkler head, he wailed until the visions were wiped out by his pain. The necklace vanished from his view as Daisy bolted and his body convulsed. Bones cracked and snapped. Muscles elongated, but Monster reeled back his shift. He would not let DIC or any one of his minor minions win or gain knowledge about his physical attributes. A FUCN'A plant.

One thing was certain. DIC had an accomplice. She was a donkey shifter. Daisy Duke was related to or associated with DIC somehow. He felt it in his bowels. Son of a silverback!

He'd caught a glimpse of Pandora's matching ruby—most likely one of the treasures she'd picked up at her B&B—which meant she'd encountered possibly DIC himself—Mrs. DIC? He needed a name and right fucking now.

One thing Monster had learned in his travels to Africa was that donkeys and gorillas had the potential to butt heads if the conditions were right.

Instead of holding on mid-shift, Monster exploded into his Lump form, the threat of the Furry Alliance Court a forgotten memory. Legs of a kangaroo, he pushed off the ground in thirty-foot bounds. He targeted the fleeing donkey, reaching her tail and narrowly missing a face punch from her back hoof.

He made his way up her body, sinking his mangled fingers into her fringed mane, and gripping it in thick wads.

She brayed and dug hooves into the soft grasses, Monster's syndactyly feet cutting two swaths in the soil as the jenny dragged him another ten feet.

He locked an arm around Daisy's neck and used her mane as leverage to slow the ass. Monster's legs hung over the back end, the tasseled tail beating his backside as he tried to drag, literally, information out of the Newbie Academy cadet. "Tell me who you are. How are you involved with DIC? I want a name. Say it, Daisy, or I'll—"

A shot rang out.

The tangled-up experimental and Daisy came to an abrupt halt, Monster's ears ringing from the blast as he retook his complete human form. He stomped a path, beelining toward his superior. "She's involved with DIC. Ask her, Alyce. Daisy, tell the director the truth."

"I'll be the one asking questions," Alyce ordered her security team to escort Daisy to the infirmary to get checked out. "Monster, get your pathetic excuse for a special ops agent outside the Academy. Now. Before I do something we are both going to regret."

Monster barely registered Alyce's pummeling lecture over his own internal voice, asking him how the Academy was tied to Dr. Crick. And why Alyce was blinded to facts. "Who the hell is DIC to you, Daisy? Tell me now or you'll be sorry."

Alyce gave Monster a shove, enforcing her will. "Leave the Academy or I'll have no choice but to see to it that your association with FUC and FUCN'A is over."

Monster picked up his clothes, his massive arms hanging to the ground as his body fought him to resume its Lump form. Fists of steel, he was pissed. He was angry at everyone and how the truth was right in front of him and had been all along—an age-old battle between species rising right here at the Academy and in the town of Willow Wisp.

Not that he could do much on his own, going after this

new lead without FUC manpower and Alyce backing him up with the big guns, protecting her students.

But Pandora?

Yes. She'd have an open mind. Wouldn't she? Even if she was blistering mad at him, she'd hear him out. He hoped. They were a team. A perfect team. Right?

Finding his truck in the parking lot, he was glad he had the means to drive. Last thing he wanted was to draw more attention to himself by doing his version of the walk of shame. He jumped behind the wheel and sped out of the Academy, hightailing it toward Pandora's house.

A yellow school bus darted in front of him.

He skidded and blared the horn. Not that it slowed the vehicle an iota. The bus had come off a side street and entered the main street, fishtailing.

What the hell was going on with this driver? He lifted a fist out the window. "Watch where you're going and slow down."

The driver found his lane, but Monster wasn't satisfied. He wanted to match a face with the license plate number and report the reckless driver. He gunned his engine, getting close to the back bumper and glass exit window.

Parker's face and hands were plastered on the back window, and his mouth was open wide in a silent scream.

Monster blinked and blinked again, the facts rolling in like a surprise tsunami. The diesel from his memories wasn't an Academy shuttle. It wasn't Alyce's personal vehi-cle. It was from the local school district. The man skimming the incoming youngsters—shifters—wasn't a FUC higher-up; he was a local, an elementary school bus driver—the same driver who had chartered Monster and most likely Willy during their early years. The same person who'd handed Pandora the flyer on a missing shifter. Only Mr.

Duke had messed with the wrong Lump-gorilla shifter this time.

He'd kidnapped Monster's son.

DIC was messing with wildfire.

Monster jammed his foot against the gas pedal, and the truck lunged forward. When his window aligned with the back of the bus, he motioned to Parker to grab hold of something and hang on tight.

Monster sped forward, catching the beady-eyed glare of the driver. What he didn't expect was to spot an unconscious Pandora. She was propped against the seat directly behind the driver. He hoped that even in her state she'd trust in him to rescue her.

The driver floored the gas, and the bus clocked out at eighty-five miles per hour.

From what Monster knew of the landscape, a T intersection was two miles ahead. That gave him less than two minutes to save his family, which forced Monster to act on Plan B.

He didn't like the option that included leaving the safety of his truck and mounting the bus. But he couldn't risk the driver getting away, as Monster's revenge for the DIC multiplied.

The driver jerked the wheel, careening the side of the bus toward the truck.

Monster yanked his wheel but then realigned with the driver. This time, he didn't see Pandora.

He wiggled off one of his shoes and wedged it to keep the gas pedal steady. He threw open the door, mounting the roof, wind making his lips flap and his eyes tear. At least he told himself it was the wind.

This was Pandora, the love of his life, and their beautiful son. A brave little boy who depended on Monster to keep them safe. But they were both in trouble if he couldn't rescue them in time before they flew over the railing up ahead and into the gorge.

He sprang forward, leaping onto the roof with a clatter, his weight denting the top.

The driver fishtailed the bus, trying to shake him, but Monster slid off the roof on the passenger side, hanging on to the frames of the open windows. DIC may have infused Monster's DNA with foreign DNA, but he could never remove the gorilla shifter from the hybrid.

Monster swung from one frame to the next, slicing his hands on the thin metal channels.

Blood trickled from the cuts, but he gritted through the pain and counted his blessings he healed fast. He tiptoed along the edge of the bus where a line of rivets gave him a way to balance as he trekked to the back of the bus.

Before he reached the rear door, he glanced inside, finding Pandora's leg sticking out from between the seats.

He didn't know if she was injured or if the driver had used other means to keep her subdued. But he wasn't taking a chance by putting himself near the business end of a possible weapon by getting close to the driver, risking Parker losing both parents.

For the first time, seeing his son's eyes red with tears, he realized he wasn't set on revenge but on getting his family to safety. Ensuring they'd never have to fear for their safety ever again. "Parker, stay with your mom," he called through an open window.

Parker darted to the front of the bus, and then he disappeared near where Pandora lay flat.

At the rear of the bus, Monster reached for the emergency door handle, giving it a hard twist and snapping it clean off.

He swung his body like a pendulum, swaying past the entrance the first time. On the second try, he was inside, his feet firmly planted on the rubber-matted floor. He had only minutes before the driver would either wrench the wheel and send the bus tipping, possibly rolling, or stay his course and drive the bus right over the cliff. "Parker," Monster called.

Pandora peeked from around one of the cushioned seats, holding Parker tight. Hope brightened her gaze. She glanced at the driver and then toward Monster. "I knew you'd come…"

As if a torpedo was targeting not only the situation but his heart, he leaped toward her, the circumstances growing even more dire when he glanced through the front window to see the yellow and black warning chevrons attached to a metal guardrail up ahead and rushing toward the bus.

Monster steeled his feet, sprouting his kangaroo legs. Gorilla arms formed, extending to reach Pandora and his son as he darted down the thin aisleway.

Her eyes widened, and she clutched Parker, seemingly frozen in place. Fearful of moving.

Maybe she didn't realize how he'd appeared or that he cared and was willing to risk his life for his family or that this maniac was driving the bus and planned on plunging them to their deaths.

Perhaps the driver had made Monster out to be the villain. Hurting his family was never on the table. He'd change his ways. He'd give up revenge for love… "You're everything to me, Pandora. You and Parker. Take my hand if you believe in us."

The driver raised a ruby necklace. "You leave this bus, and that's the last thing you'll do."

The sight of the pendant gripped Monster with memories of the agony he'd received at the hands of DIC. He couldn't be sure the driver was DIC. Monster had never seen the man. But the pendant froze him in his place as if his feet welded with the floor.

The bus crossed lanes. A car horn blared.

Monster's vision flashed to a kaleidoscope of reds.

TEN

Pandora had awakened to the vibrations of a diesel engine and her little boy's sweet hands on her face, but her floaty dreamscape was obliterated by threats of death behind her and a glorious figure that stood in front of her. At first, she thought the figure was and guardian angel holding out his massive hand. As the person came into view, she saw it was her protector. Monster held steady while she trembled, trying to come to terms that he was here to rescue her.

But after a beat and no action on Monster's part, he seemed entranced. She blinked at the offering, and even though Monster's stare seemed promising, one of resolve to rescue her and their son, something was dead wrong.

The distance between them seemed infinite. Monster was paralyzed. She didn't know if she could even stand, let alone walk to Monster and shake some sense into him. Especially with Mr. Duke waving his weapon and that damn pendant. "Monster. Monster!"

He jerked and took a shaky step forward. "Take my hand, Pandora. You can debate hating me later."

A shot rang out, the bullet piercing the cab and exiting.

Monster ducked in the nick of time. "Now."

The urgency in his voice snapped her out of the haze inflicted on her by whatever poison Mr. Duke had used in that terry cloth. She didn't hate Monster. Not in the slightest. She loved him. She'd tell him when she got the chance. But right now, with Monster back from wherever his mind had trapped him, she needed to make the best of their time.

She clutched Parker to her chest and refused to oblige Mr. Duke's command that she stay where she was while he drove wildly waving his weapon.

They crashed against a parked car, and the impact thrust Pandora and Parker into the narrow aisle.

She crab-walked toward Monster, guiding her son, protecting him with her body. When she was within reach, Monster pulled her upright, and she held on to him for dear life.

He clutched her right back, bent over, and kissed her lips. "If anything would have happened to you…"

Naturally, she kissed him back, going in for a second round. It was nothing more than a hard press of their mouths, but it was as if they were solidifying their wills to survive this wild ride and reject a future where they were not a family. She glanced behind her, but Mr. Duke white-knuckled the steering wheel.

A bird smacked the windshield.

It looked like a pigeon, leaving a dusting of feathers as the lifeless bird slid down the cracked window in slow motion.

Good gravy, they were in as much danger as anyone crossing Mr. Duke's path.

"Sit in your seat, or I'll shoot you until you're as dead as that stupid fowl." The bus veered left, and then it skated on two wheels as the driver maneuvered the corner with skilled precision. Tires squealed and pebbles from the shoulder pinged the back bumper and tire wells.

Pandora cut her scream short, fearing whether they'd make the turn or skid over the bluff. She had to stay strong for Parker, but the scent of burning rubber and smoke filled the compartment as the driver took the turn at thirty miles an hour. Even if she burst into her crow shifter form, she'd fail to save Parker. He couldn't shift yet. "Mommy's got you."

She cursed under her breath, willing a miracle to save them. Even Monster was tossed about, his hands leaving bloodied splotches on the railing.

Monster checked his pockets, dragging out his cell phone, but the glass was shattered. It seemed the cuts on his hands were already closing, as only red smudges were left behind. "I'm getting us out of here. Don't you worry, Beauty. I have a plan."

Her heart squeezed. All she could do was hang on to Parker while Monster held her, the wheels of his mind appearing to spin behind his hard glare. Her life flashed with the same impact, but all she'd struggled to understand, the importance of her choices and where life had led her, narrowed. Monster had been her hero all along. And she was important to him too.

She wrapped an arm around Monster's neck. "I'm not letting go."

He guided her and Parker closer to the edge of the back door. "You'll have to jump."

She didn't miss the fact that he was using the width of his back as a shield to protect her and their son in case the driver shot at them a second time. "I agree. If we don't and Mr. Duke stops this bus, who knows what he'll do with that gun."

"We're family. Family sticks together. We jump as soon as this beast slows." Monster used his mass, anchoring them to the high side of the bus as it continued to ride on two wheels and miraculously made the corner.

As the bus righted, it slowed even more, tipping one way and then the other, jostling the three prisoners at the back of the bus.

Monster guided her and Parker to the back of the bus, kicking the rear-exit door open.

She understood what he was doing. He was putting distance between them so he could go after the driver. In her experience, you never let a bad guy get away. He'd always return. She didn't know if Mr. Duke *was* DIC, but he wouldn't stop until he got what he wanted, which she couldn't allow. No matter what.

The impact from the front wheels hitting a metal guardrail jolted Monster backward, and he fell, landing with a *thud* on his rump as the *hisss* of brakes brought the bus to a grinding halt.

Pandora had only moments to realize that the driver had left his seat and was barreling down the aisle, weapon poised.

Monster raised up and faced the man, putting his body between them. He shouted over his shoulder, "Run, Pandora. Save our son."

Her pulse beat drums between her ears. She was helpless to protect Monster. She had to protect Parker. That was what a mother did. She protected her child—an innocent victim.

Monster wanted her to do the same—sacrifice him for his family, like he'd done all along, even if she hadn't recognized his actions until now.

It killed her to leave the man she loved behind, but she

gathered Parker, wrapped his cape around him for added protection, and leaped from the back of the bus—

Tires screeched. An incoming semi-truck blared its horn.

Pandora tucked and rolled, and the ground rose up. She crashed into the graveled roadside, her shoulder hitting first. Hugging Parker, she continued to roll, protecting him with her body to avoid becoming smashed by the collision.

Metal against metal sent sparks flying. The explosive crush of steel burst the mesh of cabs, engines, and axles into flames.

She covered her son's ears, watching the two vehicles tumble over the bluff.

A ball of orange flames licked the setting sun.

Pandora curled into a ball around her child, mumbling a string of prayers under her breath that Monster would be okay. She wasn't ready to let him go. She hadn't even formally introduced Parker to his one and only hero. She needed more time. More of every day and a long, long future.

"Where's Daddy?"

She shook her head, tears streaming down her face, unable or unwilling to utter the fact that surviving such a collision unscathed would be impossible. Even though Monster was a shifter with unique healing abilities, as she'd noted his hands had healed, no one could survive a two-hundred-foot fall and blistering flames.

Sirens sounded in the distance.

Realizing she was outside the protective walls of the Academy, she pulled Parker upright, dusting him off. It was a hard-and-fast rule that she clung to: humans were to remain in the dark in regards to shifters, and her control was slipping. "Come on. We need to leave before the police arrive."

Using her Academy training, she kept to the shadows and tree lines of town, finally entering at the back of her B&B through her garden area. The blackberry vines tripped up her already tired legs, but the dimness of early evening cast long shadows. She kept upright, lengthening her spine as best she could, projecting strength. For Parker.

When she approached the teakwood bench, she plopped down and dragged Parker into her lap, rocking him, attempting to soothe the pain in her body, heart, and mind.

What could she say to Parker? *I'm sorry I never introduced you to your father when I had the chance, and now, he's gone forever?* "I am so sorry this happened. I'm supposed to protect you, but I put us in danger by thinking we were safe walking through town when I knew there was a predator out there. I will never, ever be so wrapped up in my own thoughts that I forget that we are shifters in a human community."

"It's okay, Mommy." He swiveled in her lap and touched her face then darted off her lap and trotted to his play structure.

It was just like a child, so forgiving. Parker climbed the monkey bars she'd installed in their backyard, as if he hadn't just been kidnapped and almost taken from her forever.

Kids were resilient. Even though he'd experienced something dreadful, he wasn't letting the experience steal his joy and innocence. Yet, her tears fell. They fell until a dark shadow rolled over her. "Perfect, now a cloud..."

"I've never been called a cloud, beauty."

At the sound of Monster's voice, she sprang from her seat and flew into his arms. He was covered in soot and dirt, but from what she could tell, he wasn't burned or broken. She kissed his cheeks, his forehead, his mouth, and would have continued if a storm of questions hadn't rolled in. "How? How did you survive that fall? Is Mr. Duke DIC? Is he dead? Can we go on with our lives?"

Monster lifted her until her feet dangled. He kissed her again, as if assuring her that he was in fact immortal and would never leave her again.

"That pigeon saved my life by cracking the windshield," he finally answered. "When the semi hit, I was slammed against the pane and found myself on the ground as the vehicles missed me by inches. Mr. Duke is most definitely working with DIC but I believe as an accomplice. I think DIC is someone with an animal science degree who specializes in genetics. I was able to make it to the wreckage and pull out the driver of the semi. He'll survive. But the bus driver vanished."

He didn't answer her last question. But the answer was obvious. Their lives were in limbo until DIC was captured. "In his condition, Mr. Duke couldn't have gotten far."

Monster righted his torn shirt. "Either way, he or whomever he's working for is not going to let this go…"

Pandora stole a kiss that lingered and warmed her up inside. She had to make the most of every moment. Monster must have agreed. He wrapped an arm around her back, cinching them together, and she knew it was time for him to meet his son. "Can you sit and wait here?"

"Ah, suuuure?" Monster tested the edge of the worn wooden bench.

Of course, Monster was caught off guard by her insistence that he take a seat. But some conversations were meant to be had seated. She made her way to Parker "Can you come here? I need you to meet someone who is very important in your life."

Hanging upside down on the bars, Parker gazed up at

her quizzically before glancing at the bench, his plaid cape brushing the shredded bark. He dropped to all fours and then skipped to her, jumping up and down. "Daddy's home. I knew he'd come."

She took up his hand, squeezing it gently. She wished she could have been as sure as her child's innocent mind that Monster would stay. That he wouldn't be recaptured or killed. That Parker wouldn't be made into a chimera as Monster had been. DIC was still out there; she felt that in her bones.

Her lip quivered, but she tamped down her fears, her sense of release that they'd escaped death blanketing her with peace. For now. Today was about a reunion that should have happened the moment she found out she was pregnant. She'd stolen time from Monster, from herself, from their son. She released Parker's hand.

He jetted toward Monster, coming up short when he stared up at the imposing figure. He held out his hand, a hand dwarfed by his dad's. "I'm Parker Monster Johnson."

His hand floated midair, and both looked each other over.

Pandora held her breath, hoping Monster approved of her son's middle name. She'd taught her son formal greetings in the presence of strangers due to her B&B. Repeat customers praised her manners and that of her sometimes–rambunctious four-year-old. But this introduction was precious, even as moments passed.

A tear leaked from Monster's eye. He dropped to his knees, enveloped his son's hand, and the two gripped each other.

Soft sobs from Monster sounded around the father and son.

The sweetest and most forgiving sound Pandora had ever hoped for in their reunion.

Monster lifted his face from the crook of Parker's neck. He waved her over.

This was all she'd wanted—her family together in a place they could call home for the rest of their lives. A family built on acceptance, compassion, and love. She snuggled in, the three of them planting roots in the welcoming garden soil.

"I'm home, you two. If you'll have me." Monster eased both of them back.

She told herself to be careful. It wasn't only her heart on the line. It was Parker's.

But love wasn't easy. Love was blind acceptance of Monster's pure heart but also his career.

Their relationship was all-encompassing. When it came to the three of them, even if Monster left again, and he would, they would get through the hard parts of life in his absence. "We still have jobs to do before we settle down. Even a four-year-old knows bad men don't stay put."

"Mommy, I'm hungry."

She patted Parker on the head, motioning to the jungle gym. "Go play a little longer. I'll bring dinner."

Monster stayed with Parker, keeping an ever-watchful eye.

Pandora whipped up Parker's favorite fruit salad with a heap of berries from her garden, bananas, guava, and a hot bowl of homemade mac and cheese. She took the food out to the garden table, draping a cloth over the rustic wood, and setting the place settings. She even lit a citronella candle to keep any mosquitoes away. But even though bliss surrounded them, trouble weighed heavy in the air, the smoke of the burning collision making its way clear across town.

"This is beautiful, beauty." Taking the offered napkin, Monster sat beside Parker. "I'm starving."

"I don't know why. We ate pizza only twenty-four hours ago," she joked, her smirk strained.

"It seemed like a lifetime ago when we rekindled. I wish I hadn't waited so long." Monster dug his spoon into the macaroni and filled his mouth, chewing around his words. "Best meal I've ever had in my life."

His words were full of meaning, emotions, and love. But what Pandora realized as they ate, cleaned up, showered, settled in for the night, and finally tucked Parker into bed was that it wasn't only Monster who'd felt like he'd come home. It was her.

She slid beside her man in bed, wrapping a leg across his hips as they snuggled under the covers. She found him reaching for her. Kissing her, the mattress a pillowy cushion for their sprains and abrasions. She knew she'd held back her feelings. But the deeper Monster kissed her, the deeper she fell in love, the deeper their bond fused...

The more she had to lose. Against his lips, she breathed, "I love you, Monster."

ELEVEN

Monster woke at the sound of shattering glass. He sprang upright. Patting the bed, he found Pandora sitting as well. Both tried to come to terms with where the abrupt noise that felt as if it shook the house had come from. It wasn't a gunshot. He was certain of that. Nor was it someone within the home milling about in the early-morning hours; it wasn't any normal night sound. He didn't waste another moment thinking about the cause. "I think I heard glass breaking. Stay here."

"I'm going with you." Pandora hopped out of bed, wrapped a robe around herself, and slipped on house shoes. She crossed to the adjoining room, having shared her bed with Parker, making sure that he was tucked in bed. "He's asleep."

Monster's tension lessened a hair. No use wasting time discussing his next move. He tossed on pants, Pandora having cleaned and dried them the night before. At least he had a barrier to protect him should he come face-to-face with a human. His body wasn't put together as nature had intended—even before he'd become a Lump, his shifted, four-hundred-pound size was imposing—and he didn't need anyone asking questions. "Stay behind me."

"Will do."

With Pandora playing backup, Monster scanned the hallway, a soft glow from the sconces lighting a path. He didn't know the layout of the home well, but the front door was still locked. He padded in bare feet past the foyer and the dining room. The tulips he'd purchased the day before had partially closed in the dimness of the early morning, but the panoramic window was still intact. "How many other rooms?"

"Only one downstairs. It isn't being used. The rest are upstairs, but I only have two rooms housing single guests at the moment. I'm the only one with a key after hours."

Monster listened for movement upstairs, dumbfounded no one had made it downstairs. "Show me the rest of the house."

Pandora placed her hand on his back, the pressure guiding him forward "Is DIC here? Mr. Duke? Has someone come to retaliate after this afternoon? He's never going away."

He didn't want to add to her nerves. "Let's not jump to conclusions."

"Probably a good idea," Dora whispered.

Acute to his surroundings, he made his way into the kitchen, making sure a guest hadn't dropped a canister in the kitchen. He wasn't sure where the sound had come from, but it had been louder and larger than a shattering glass cup. Although the noise seemed close, or at least within the downstairs portion of the home, he'd been half asleep.

"Another note," Pandora shrilled.

Written on the outside of the kitchen window in

bamboo shoots, which Pandora grew in the garden as a screen along one side of her yard, was another message. This one was much more menacing than the first. It read: *The old red barn. Come alone.*

Monster's pulse flooded his veins at the display. The cat-and-mouse chase had become a dangerous game. Still, he tried to play off his perspiration and grinding jaw with a lighthearted comment. "Seems like the man likes to play with his food."

"It's not his food I'm worried about." Pandora wrung her hands. "You can't go alone to meet him. Not after what happened today. Mr. Duke is murderous, deranged, if this is him. If you disappear, I'll never know what happened to you. I'm coming with you. Somehow. Some way."

He didn't know if Mr. Duke was DIC's accomplice until Pandora had shared the last words she'd remembered hearing before she'd passed out. Mr. Duke was working for DIC in some capacity. In his gut, he felt that one of DIC's accomplices would appear if they had the chance, and Monster wasn't wrong. But who was this individual exactly? What did they really want from Monster, and what was his motivation? He felt played, possibly deceived, but he couldn't grasp who had toyed with his family and why. His view of the answers blurred.

"The final conversation I had with the driver before I was expelled from the belly of the bus proved the man wasn't giving up easily. Especially since DIC knows of Parker."

"That means they won't stop until they're either behind bars or dead." Pandora covered her chest with both hands.

Pandora was right. This grudge seemed to be one species upping another and longing to be the bigger ass.

Unfortunately, only DIC knew the true motivation and end game.

Pandora kicked a decorative pillow, the trajectory narrowly missing Monster. She let out a maddening wail, feathers sprouting from the material seams in an angry display of pillow mutilation. "He can't have our son."

The disruption of her sleep and threat seemed to be driving her mad, as if DIC was winning already. Which Monster tried to calm. "By mutating gorilla shifters into dysfunctional parts and attempting to shorten their lives, mutated DNA could transfer to gorilla offspring to water down as many gorilla shifters as possible. Only Parker was conceived before I was mutated. Once DIC learns this, he could change his mind about wanting our child."

"There are too many unknowns. That doesn't make me feel better. We don't know what DIC's plans are. Perhaps what's driving him is the twisted ego of one man who gained a following and then poisoned them with magical tea. We can't really know the workings of madness."

Monster scoffed at his and Pandora's ponderings, but his anger tripled. If DIC had taken a good look at his victims —at Monster—he'd have seen that Monster was more like a donkey in that he didn't easily travel in a direction he didn't think was right.

That little voice inside of Monster, one of familial loyalty, had been there all along, telling him that home was where his loved ones lived, which included Pandora and Parker.

Like a donkey, he'd persevered. He'd finished one grueling mission after another, making sure the furry innocent were protected. Yet he identified with the gorillas as well. He was a gentle healer, a protector to the core, powerful both physically and mentally as he had gone up against Crick the first time he'd escaped, even blinded and paralyzed by that gem.

Nothing had changed. Not really. Except that DIC had met Parker. Perhaps it wasn't the mutation he was after but the lifespan Monster had achieved.

Monster pivoted, meeting Pandora's gaze. "Go check on our son. Stay with him until I find out what's going on outside. Someone could still be trespassing."

Pandora hesitated briefly before trotting back the way they came.

Monster proceeded, pushing open the last downstairs door—

The French doors were wide open, the molding splintered, and several panes had been smashed in.

He flicked on the light.

Pandora screamed from behind him near their adjoined first-floor bedrooms, the high pitch waking the house. Upstairs, footsteps trotted around and creaked the first-floor ceiling.

His worst nightmares rushed in on him, stealing his breath as he found Pandora clutching Parker's cape.

"He never takes off his cape. Never." She gripped his arms. "He's been abducted."

The monster caught a glimpse of Pandora's necklace on the bedside table and swooped it up in his hand without staring at the trance-inducing item. She'd taken it off since she and Parker were sharing her bed. She didn't realize the danger of the stone or its hypnotic effects on him. "Where did you get this?"

"Ms. Epona left it here. She only stayed for one night. I had such a day yesterday that I completely forgot it was in my pocket when I talked with her—"

She let her words fade but then continued, her tone

clinging to a frantic pitch. "Ms. Epona was having construction done to her house, which isn't exactly a traditional home. Monster, it's the red barn at the edge of town. You know, the one that rescues equines and attempts to compete with ARSHOL. The equine rescue and charity. Tootsie has lived there with her father for years. Good heavens— He's a retired zoologist who specialized in genetics."

Monster didn't flinch. He didn't budge. He gripped the pendant until it crumbled in his hands. "I had checked out the place, initially. Right after I escaped. I told FUC authorities and Alyce that the farm had a scent of old straw dust and alfalfa, sweet—medical. It was the only place I got gooseflesh when I drove by. Literally."

Pandora's eyes sprang wide as he patted the gooseflesh erupting on his forearms.

She slipped off her robe. "Willy mentioned it as well. It's why we suspected carrot-loving Alyce. I'm surprised the woman's skin isn't tinged orange from carotenemia."

Monster recalled the conversion he'd had with Alyce, BS, and his superiors after he'd escaped. No one had believed him when he'd suggested the rescue owner, the sweet principal of Willow Wisp high school, four years prior. "The barn must be the place, perhaps a bunker that we missed. But Alyce is done with me. We're on our own."

Pandora kicked off her house shoes. "The farm is a hop, skip, and a jump for you, but I think you better drive my car since your truck isn't here. Can't have you shifting for the whole town to see. And DIC may be looking for you. For me, it's a five-minute flight."

Her tone fueled him. He felt deceived by both Alyce and Tootsie, the principal of his high school, now Parker's elementary school. And Pandora was right about his truck, the poor thing totaled at the side of the road. "Tootsie knows as much about me as she does our son. Everything."

"She has tested him regularly, both physically and mentally. Parker is gifted, and she's aware he's special. She's even invited us to her farm. To think that she was making me out to be a bad mother and had an agenda all along." She stamped her foot. "I'm enraged and considering revenge. Someone had planned to harm our child. But Karma is a vengeful bitch, and she's showing up as a wicked crow shifter today."

Before Monster could comment, Pandora shifted, letting out a shrill cry and flapping her wings as she flew out of her bedroom, down the hallway, past the kitchen, and out of the bedroom's broken French doors. The fight of their lives was upon them.

Monster wasn't far behind her, although her car seemed somewhat dwarfed with him behind the wheel, and he struggled working the floor pedals, as he had the night they'd broken into the Academy. When he reached the red barn, he parked near the front mailbox. Surprising the father-daughter duo, who expected them, wasn't necessary.

With a birds-eye view, Pandora was already checking the property from the roof, noting the grazing burros and a couple of mules eating spring grasses. The place looked majestic cast upon the mountain-scape in the distance. But Monster wasn't fooled.

Apparently, neither was Pandora, who readied for a brawl and sharpened her beak on the iron rooster weather-vane. She took flight and darted inside the lower level of the home, the portion that resembled a barn-shop combination, doing reconnaissance of the open level.

Monster couldn't have been prouder at how she'd remembered her training, which seemed like a lifetime from where they were now. But it was like learning how to ride a bike—it came naturally.

Monster slithered along the corrugated siding, ducking when he came to a window. He listened for signs of occupancy, but hearing only the ruffle of Pandora's feathers, he entered the lower level.

A truck sat empty to one side, its exhaust pipe littered with rusted holes, but under the vehicle was a clean metal panel—a basement bulkhead door.

He needed Pandora to watch his back. Fearing calling for her, he slipped back out from where he came and tucked his mass between two stacks of straw.

Pandora continued to scout the upper levels of the home, perching on the outside window boxes, where she plucked at the geraniums angrily.

The stone came out of nowhere, knocking her off the planter.

Monster punched upright but forced himself to remain hidden.

She squealed and flapped her wings as she tumbled downward but righted herself.

Monster clutched his tight chest, unwilling to admit how close she'd come to getting beaned a second time.

Movement caught his eye near the barn opening, both sliding doors held open in their channels.

It was an older gentleman. Monster hadn't been in town in a while, but not much had changed. It was a small town, and he'd never seen the man. Not one time. At least not with a rotund belly, glasses, and a ruby hanging from his neck chain.

A silhouette formed in his mind, one he overlaid against the older man.

Holy Sacred Headwaters. Images rushed through

Monster's mind. The man who'd tortured him had changed. He was wrinkled around the eyes and lips, dark spots dotted his complexion as if he'd spent long hours under the damaging sun. The man no longer looked like the youthful man who'd stood beside him in the horrible photo Pandora had seen in his file, taken four years prior. It was as if DIC's practices had shredded him into pieces and rearranged *his* bone structure and facial expressions so that his emotions and the lines that should have been created over time were scribbled on his face. As if DIC had exponentially aged. As if DIC himself was broken. As if DIC could be taken down.

Pandora dove, striking the man's balding head.

Her kind was known to aggressively defend their nests. She dive-bombed him again. A relentless attack of squawking and pecking that proved she could fight a fair fight.

Monster smiled, and his vengeful goal took shape.

DIC swatted and then sprinted for the barn's interior.

The click of the shotgun stopped Monster.

In mid-flight, Pandora thrust her wings forward as she backpedaled to safety. She descended, tucking her wings to her body to make use of the air foiling around her teardrop shape, giving her stealth and speed.

Monster crouched between the bales, studying the animals in the field and recognizing one who held her head up high. Another who lay sprawled out in the grasses, unmoving—Mr. Duke, he suspected had made it to the equine rescue before collapsing and dying. He suspected the donkey army was lying in wait for a signal of some kind.

Another shot rang out.

Buckshot raced past Pandora, but she darted out of the way of the lead beads. When she touched down beside him, she took a full minute to catch her breath. Hiding behind a haystack, she transformed. "We're gonna need a murder or a miracle to take down DIC and his drove of donkeys."

He scooted her way, wishing she did have a flock of crow shifters to back her and knowing that she'd traded friends of a feather to raise their son. "Pandora. I'm here. You're amazing. I'm not giving up yet."

She twisted, facing Monster. "Your skin is straw-colored and blends into the dry grass so perfectly it's like you have chameleon DNA."

"Could be." He passed her a sweater, the one she'd left in the car the night they'd found the banana note. It wasn't any longer than thigh-length, but it was protection from human eyes should any have witnessed her shifting as they drove past the farm. "Better put this on to keep passers-by from calling out human police for a potential 5150 and an indecent exposure charge or the damn COOCHI."

"Good idea. Last thing we need is the chaos brought on by the Corrective Outdoor Shifter or Calming of Humans Incident team. But listen. DIC has a shotgun, and he's protecting a hidden space under the truck. There could be chimeras waiting, compelled by the stone to do DIC's bidding. I need to get inside and rescue Parker, and I think you're best up against the herd."

DIC was plotting backup, and Monster was taking him down. It was a given. "Saw the trap door and got a whiff of Parker's scent."

"Me too," she croaked.

Monster released a heavy sigh, knowing he'd have to face his biggest fear, which was reentering the space he'd been experimented on. But first, he'd have to deal with DIC, as Pandora had suggested. She didn't have the skills he carried or the expertise to fight off multiple attackers. "FYI. Those equines in the field aren't pets. They're DIC's army, minus the deceased jack. I believe that is… was Mr. Duke. Worse, I recognize one of my students."

"Who?" Pandora's brows tipped toward her hairline.

"The donkey shifter, of course. Daisy Duke has anger issues. Now I know why, living in these poor conditions. Not much of a barn, drafty stalls, and moldy feed. It's not uncommon for orphaned shifters to be found mingling among the non-shifting. I can't believe the SPCA or the county animal control isn't on top of this. Or MUFF, since they're on the lookout for the unethical treatment of non-sentient animals by shifters."

"The Merrily United Furry Friends have an impossible job, as do the others. They can't be everywhere, especially since this property is protected by a boundary of street trees."

Before Monster could respond, the sound of thunderous hooves erupted from the field, and high-pitched braying echoed inside the barn.

Pandora made fists. "An army of donkey shifters? This is unexpected. But I can take them."

Monster dragged her back into the mountain of bales. "I know you can, but we have to play this smart and are out of time. You have my back. I'll enter the barn and move that truck. Then I'll deal with DIC. Force him to administer the cure. By now, he has to have come up with an antidote… You find Parker and beat it out of here. Keys are under the seat. And I tucked his cape into your empty sweater pocket."

Pandora let a tear slip, feeling the mound through her cashmere. "I know you'll *deal* with DIC. But I hope you don't do to him what he did to you, or worse. Do the right thing. Make the decision to let go of the past if given the option, okay?"

Revenge brewed inside him, burning hot in his belly,

and he was certain Pandora picked up on his taste for it. "I'll do my best."

"I'll go after Parker and deal with Tootsie. She's mine. All mine."

"I like it when you're fired up. I plan to show you how much as soon as I take down DIC and administer the cure." Monster branded her lips with his then sprinted, his mass pounding a path in the muck toward the barn.

CHAPTER
TWELVE

Pandora's arms ached, but she shifted once more, clutching the sweater with her talons. This was her son. She would expend every bit of energy to save her little Monster. Together they had this. She wing-punched the air in celebration and flew back toward the barn, noting the drove of donkeys were held back by strings of rusted barbed-wire and half-chewed cedar fence posts. She didn't have much time before the donkey army toppled the fence. But strangely, it was as if someone was keeping them from thinking and shifting on their own and opening the gate.

A sharp blast from a weapon punched a hole the size of a watermelon in the side of the barn, shards of wood exploding into Pandora's airspace just as an engine gasped for life, died, and then rumbled, tires finding purchase on the straw-laden barn floor.

"*Shriek!*" Pandora remembered the sound of the truck that had left the pizzeria parking lot. It had to be the same ramshackle vehicle, as the tinny exhaust sound was distinguishable from any other truck. She gained altitude to check the barn and the push of donkeys before entering.

Whew. Monster and the older man wrestled with the shotgun, but Monster was on top.

She *caw-cawed* and took her human shape upon landing near the relocated truck, her skin gathering a sticky sheen from shifting too many times in a row. She threaded on her sweater, buttoning the middle button to keep the thing closed. Straining until her eyes bulged like a Potoo bird's, she managed to raise the hatch. She trotted down a flight of well-lit steps, cautious of a surprise attack.

Parker was sitting at a kiddy table, coloring with Tootsie, as if they didn't have a care in the world and were deaf to the debacle upstairs. The room was lined with stainless-steel tables, and several stalls had chains and cuffs mounted to a labyrinth of metal frames. The scene was right out of the files she'd found in Monster's file and studied at FUCN'A when she was a cadet.

Pandora's heart, all the pieces that Monster had somehow managed to piece back together in the last two days, threatened to break all over again from the horrors she imagined happening within this room. Even Daisy Duke had perhaps been cowed into submission and forced to take up a defensive pose. "Let my son go."

"Your son?" Tootsie patted Parker on the head, as if he were an obedient retriever.

The nerve. Pandora balled her hands and snapped her jaw, forgetting that she'd lost her beak in the transforma-tion. "Yes. He may be in your care for three hours a day, but he's mine. My flesh and blood. Monster's son."

Tootsie clicked her tongue and strolled around the metal bed, lifting and dropping the restraints. "Monster's trans-formation happened right here in this very room. It's been that way for years. Testing. Seeing who lives and dies. Tweaking the formulas to see if I can extend the lives of the chimeras. Finding a cure. Of course, neither has been possible. Until Monster showed up in town. I heard it from one of my spies."

Yes, of course. Alyce had asked Monster to monitor her students. At first, Monster had suspected Willy was a plant. "Daisy. We've met."

"That's right. See, it was not my father, Ichabod, who took credit for the original testing. Not really. I pressured him after I lost my husband to the trials. My father wanted the best for his daughter. He tried to fix me. But I couldn't live in a town where I was the only naturally-born chimera. I've grown lonely. My goals have changed as of late."

Pandora watched as Tootsie's eyes glossed over and then refocused on Parker.

"See, I wanted a child. Parker has Monster's blood in him. Chimera DNA. My DNA. He's bound to live a long, long life. He's as much mine as he is—"

"Take it back," Pandora blurted out. Tootsie was spinning the conversation in an objectionable direction. Parker was pure as a gorilla-crow could be. Conceived before Monster's genetics had been compromised.

Perhaps Tootsie read Pandora's expression, learning the truth.

Tootsie's arms twitched, and her facial features contorted. Her nose slid to where her right ear had been, the ear disappearing completely. Two eyes combined to one. Where her fingers were, tentacles formed, suction cups engulfing her nail beds. Where her legs once stood, giraffe legs appeared, kneeless.

Parker screamed, crawled between Tootsie's misshapen knees, and dashed to Pandora.

She gripped her son to her waist. He wasn't a small child, but she managed to backtrack, keeping eyes on

Tootsie as she observed the woman gritting through one horrific change after another—a potent Lump herself.

Pandora had no idea what the woman left unsaid, but perhaps her father had tried to perfect a mate, who, one after the other, fell short and died.

Except for Monster. Is that why she'd initially made Willy? To entice Monster back to town, and then used Parker to recapture his father? What about this other teen who was reported missing?

Hooves beat toward Pandora, and she took the stairs two at a time, reaching the last step—

Tootsie gripped Pandora's leg. "*Reviens ici salope.*"

The foreign, high-pitched squeal blasted in Pandora's ears, but she knew French when she heard it. And, *bitch*, she wasn't coming back. Not anytime soon.

She spilled Parker onto the upper level, kicked at Tootsie's hold, and wrenched her body, twisting and thrashing on the ground floor.

Tootsie jerked Pandora down one step and then another.

Pandora kept eye contact with Parker. The boy didn't cowl. He peered over at the brawl between his daddy and DIC. "Use the cape, Mommy. It has superpowers."

She dug in her pocket, finding a portion of the cape had escaped. Using a free hand, she found the trinkets she'd picked up from the pizzeria in the other pocket. She had one shot. Once she let go of the step she clung to, Tootsie would drag her down. No telling what would happen.

She took the material and twirled it, as if she were holding two ends of a jump rope. Then she wound up and let one end fly as she slid down the steps on her rump.

Sure enough, Tootsie fell backward, end over end, the cloth having zapped her in her cyclops' eyeball.

Crash!

Donkeys rushed the barn. It was two against what felt like a million.

The donkeys charged, stirring up dust and fine strands of brittle hay.

Pandora raced up the steps and closed the trapdoor, shutting Tootsie inside. She didn't know how long she had until Tootsie regained her eyesight and strength, but Pandora used the time wisely. She bolted toward Parker, shoved the cape into his hands, and ordered him to lock himself inside the truck's cab. "Stay here. Don't come out until the coast is clear."

The donkeys circled, blowing up debris, flashing teeth, ears pinned to their manes.

DIC might have aged, but he was as strong as a mule. He threw a sucker punch that sent Monster reeling.

Pandora limped, and her body felt like roadkill. She had one last shift in her. Maybe two. To save her man, she put her faith in him to stay down long enough for her to take out some dirty asses. For her, for Parker. Monster had to choose to put his faith in the one person who'd had his back.

As bad as it looked, it was her.

She stripped off her sweater, set it against the barn wall, and shifted back into her crow shape. She flew toward the rafters before diving and landing on the bald crest of DIC's forehead, going for the eyes. *Peck, peck, peck.*

One of the donkeys charged, kicking up her back end and swatting the crow shifter with her tail, as if Pandora were a bug who'd taken a beating with the business end of a fly swatter.

Pandora crashed against the far wall, little white lights dancing around her feathered head.

The donkey reared and pawed at Monster, who crawled to standing.

Pandora gave a harsh, repeating *caw*. Monster was a beast, his body akin to a ball of raw dough rather than the bird-gorilla-kangaroo shifter she'd seen at the Academy. His beastly limbs stuck out at odd angles. But underneath his doughy exterior, she knew his heart. And she loved him. Unable to hold on to her shift, her human form poured onto the ground. "You got this, Monster. Now let's take 'em down."

That gorilla gene woven through Monster's DNA must have heard her because a row of silver hairs dappled the ridge of Monster's backside, and black hairs sprouted along his thick shoulders, creating a dense-haired forest. His arms sprang from his sides, retook their gorilla form, fingers and all, as if Monster was gaining clarity and showing the world that he wasn't going down without a fight.

Donkeys flew as, one after the other, Monster sent their bodies toward the trussed ceiling. But as they crashed into the ground, they reanimated and charged, forcing him to fight, even as they kicked him when he was down.

The hatch blew open, and Tootsie the kraken emerged.

Pandora shared a look of defeat with Monster, but it was brief. She had Parker to think about. "Watch out!"

Sirens wailed, and tires slid on gravel outside the barn.

Alyce was the first to round the corner, weapons in both hands, along with FUC agents, and a welcomed cadet by the name of Willy Tagger. Then it rained.

Tranquilizer darts sprayed the interior, but one donkey took off and jumped when it reached the opening to the basement. Willy gave chase.

Pandora darted to her sweater. She rummaged through the weighted pocket, finding the parmesan shaker and packets of chili peppers. No way could she allow DIC to escape or hurt another.

Even with darts sticking out of Tootsie's throat, the woman still managed to wrestle Monster, who dragged the powerful Lump down the flight of stairs where, Pandora suspected, donkey DIC had descended.

She twisted off the lid, tore open one packet after the other of chili flakes, and poured the contents into the container. Then, leaving the sweater for later, she prayed she could shift a second last time.

Skin sprouted feathers, her arms became wings, and using her powerful legs, she propelled herself upward, gripping the shaker. If she positioned herself just right—

"I'll kill you, Monster." DIC cursed. "You killed my cousin."

Mr. Duke? Well, that tied up that loose end. Pandora swooped down the stairs, taking note of the offense Alyce seemed to be leading.

Apparently suffering the effects of the darts, the remaining donkey shifters wove a drunken trail toward the barn's shiplap siding. They flailed, brayed, and lost their shifter forms, exposing their true identities.

"Go get 'em, super mom." Parker cheered from the cab, waving his cape.

Pandora had always wanted to become an agent and take out the bad guys. And now she had the encouragement of her child telling her to kick some DIC ass. And she did.

Faster than she'd ever flown, knowing her son was rooting for her, she sailed toward Monster, who was matching punch for kick with Tootsie, while DIC was working the lock on one of his refrigerated glass cabinets and fighting off Willy, who'd entered the fray.

Exchanging punches, the foursome locked in a battle of fists, tentacles, paws, and hooves of fury.

Corone help her. Pandora joggled the glass jar in her hooked claws, having half the contents to her benefit. Only one last move to take down the enemies who'd hurt her family.

With her powerful pizza condiment concoction, she let it snow.

Monster shoved Willy from harm's way.

Red pepper flakes and crumbled parmesan fell into DIC's and Tootsie's eyes, sending DIC braying and scrambling to remove the burn of chili flakes from sensitive features. DIC kicked air and struck the pharmaceutical cabinet labeled Cure.

Tootsie deflated like a year-old pumpkin, her skin shriveling about her innards. She pulled herself toward the vial. "It's mine. It's mine…"

Monster landed a foot on her arm, crushing it along with a few jewels that had fallen from a table onto the floor. "I don't think so. This is the cure. It's what I need to get my life back. Years that both of you stole from me."

Pandora landed and took her human form. She divided her gaze between Willy, who was chaining DIC to the restraining mechanism, and Monster who held the cure. But the cure to what? Surely, if Tootsie was after the cure, she hadn't found it. "Monster, I love you. I don't care what you look like when you shift. I care about who you are as a mate, a lover, and a father. You're an amazing agent. Look at Willy. You gave him the courage to face his fears, fears I know you have inside of you. But look at the degree Tootsie and her father went to morph their appearances to their ideal of perfection. No one is perfect. We have to learn to love ourselves, inside and out. In their hunt for perfection, they've gone mad. I don't want that for you."

"Neither do I." Alyce came up behind her, chewing on a strand of crimped alfalfa and passing Dora her sweater, which Pandora put on. "I was wrong to doubt you, Monster. Your instincts have never wavered. No change in DNA distorted the hero I know, who your mom knew, and the man I've come to call friend."

The vial shook in Monster's hand, and he twisted off the cap, holding the ruby liquid in the air. Only this time, he didn't freeze or blank out. The potion wasn't like the jewels smashed on the basement floor—yet it seemed to have some kind of power over him.

"Monster..." Pandora pleaded. "Do the right thing."

"I've hated you, DIC." Monster lifted the vial to his lips. "I've wished you dead more times than I can count. I've prayed you wouldn't take another shifter to torture and to watch die. But thinking I would ever join your games is over. I won't let myself down by choosing revenge. I won't let anger control my life. Not when I have so much to live for. We have top scientists who will study and find a cure. Maybe in time, Willy, and other chimeras like him, will gain the opportunity to find their way back to the shifter they were before you changed them. But for me, I'm happy with who I am. Inside and out. Pandora and my son made me see the truth."

"Daddy." Parker swung from the railings and leaped into his daddy's arms. "You are the best fighters ever, you and Mommy, but where's your cape?"

Monster cracked a smile and hugged his son as he passed the vial to Alyce. "There should be another gorilla shifter on-site."

"Found him. He's okay and wasn't experimented on."

Alyce motioned for the agents to enter, other heroes like Monster and Pandora. "COOCHI is on the way…"

Pandora's tension poured out of her. In her eyes, the FUC agents and Monster didn't need capes to prove they were good guys, and there were many. "Ready to go home?"

Monster decorated Willy with a look of utter gratitude and approval and gathered Pandora's hand, kissing her knuckles. "I'm ready to follow you wherever you go."

"I'm hungry," Parker protested. "I want pizza for lunch."

Pandora laughed and nuzzled into Monster's side. She didn't stop smiling. Not as they were buckled into their seats, having adorned the spare clothes she'd received from NAKED, the Network for Apparel and Kit Express Delivery she'd found waiting for them in her car. Nor as they put miles between the barn and their messy pasts, both looking to the horizon and open roadway.

Pandora was certain Monster was and had always been her man, her everything. Lump or not, she loved him with her whole being. They were a family with nothing but the future ahead of them, and she deserved the rest of the day and night off. The B&B guests could give her a one-star rating if they expected a home-cooked meal later tonight. "Actually, I'm craving pizza, too."

No one would ever separate them again. And that was a promise she'd uphold.

Her cell dinged, and Pandora read the text. "It's Alyce already. She says Parker is a shoo-in at the Academy after he graduates from high school. She says she's signing off on the completion of my Conflict Resolution Class and welcomes me to walk with the spring graduating class."

Pandora paused and pushed back happy tears. "And she wants to know if *we're* available to talk about teaching the coping class together. That is, if we're not asked to work a future FUC mission as a cohesive pair. Says she'd back us with her approval, and we make a good team if asked."

"She never stops..." Monster groaned and took the phone from her hand, keeping one hand on the wheel. He set the device face down after clicking off the ringer. "But she cares and loves us. I love her too. Mom would be proud of what we just accomplished as a team effort."

Pandora agreed wholeheartedly. At the core, she and Monster were both protectors of the innocent. There were classes to teach, a child to raise, a B&B to run, a graduation to attend, missions waiting, and crimes against the furry to solve. Pandora knew in her heart they'd both reconnect with the FUC at some level. But not today. "Alyce is tenacious. But it's because she cares passionately for her students, newbies, and graduates of all ages. For now, *I* want to focus on loving you. I want you to get to know our son."

Monster brushed a cheese crumb from her cheek, adding a smirk that crinkled his eyes. "You do plan on replacing the parm shaker, right?"

She spread a mischievous grin on her face as she found a parking space, Parker ditching them for a sprint inside the pizzeria arcade. She accepted her nature. Always had and always would. There were adventures to be had, collections to be gathered, treasures to be rediscovered in a chimera called Monster. She cooed, "The only thing I'm stealing is your heart."

Monster leaned across the console and kissed her, letting their lips reacquaint with the dance they'd choreographed years ago. "It's yours, Pandora. My heart and soul. Forever. Always."

She believed him.

The End

Find out what happens to FUCN'A cadet Willy Tagger, who's hot on the tail of a sexy hairball-leaving, feral-feline shifter in Chimera and the Cat Burglar, coming soon!

And there are more FUC Academy books by other authors coming soon!

To find out more, visit worlds.EveLanglais.com or stay in the loop with our newsletter. Sign up at subscribepage.com/evelworlds

ABOUT THE AUTHOR

 *USA Today* Bestselling Author of The Faeted Vampire Series, Cyndi Faria writes steamy paranormal vampire, werewolf, & shifter romance with twist-turns you'll never see coming and happily-ever-after endings you crave. Recently, she found her passion writing zany paranormal cozies, which makes sense since her bookaholic, swearing-like-a-sailor momma taught her that silliness and shenanigans make the world a happy place.

When this California girl isn't nose-deep in a romance book, she's walking the beach, snuggling on the couch with her rescued furbabies, sipping tea, and binging on the newest paranormal release, *Vampire Diaries* reruns or her guilty pleasure, *The Bachelor*!

Website: cyndifaria.com

Newsletter Signup: dl.bookfunnel.com/h6jfaiaz77

Facebook Group Cyndi's Superstars: facebook.-com/groups/398472573898406/

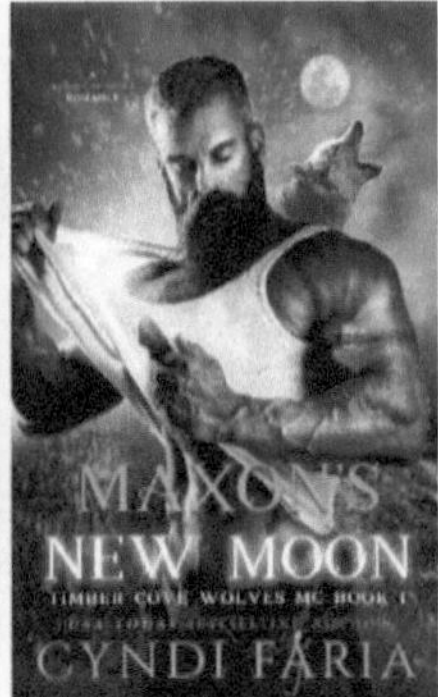

facebook.com/CyndiFariaAuthor

instagram.com/cyndifaria

tiktok.com/@authorcyndifaria

bookbub.com/authors/cyndi-faria

Also by Cyndi Faria

CHIMERA AND THE CAT BURGLAR

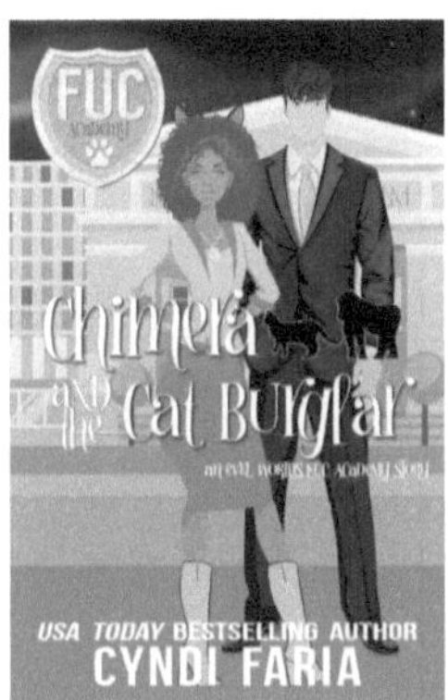

Can these exes recover a stolen artifact, or will the kitty make off with the prize?

Someone's stolen the golden phallus! As witnesses to the covert crime on campus, Willy Tagger, must team up with his slinky cat shifter ex to catch the slippery burglar.

Boo Bombay wanted to see the artifact returned to its rightful home, but before she could steal it and return it to her family, someone beat her to it! Now she'll have to keep the heat off by working with Willy to find it. But when they do track it down, will she return it to the Academy, or keep it for herself?

There isn't a lock Willy can't open, but he's pulling out hairs trying to pick Boo's guarded heart. It doesn't help that Boo's scaled in secrets.

They might have a chance if these exes can battle their lust-hate relationship and avoid the spellbinding pull of the artifact.

www.ingramcontent.com/pod-product-compliance
Lightning Source LLC
Chambersburg PA
CBHW021447150726

47989CB00001B/433